Champions
of
Pleasure

A Novel by
Gloria G. Brame

Moons Grove Press
British Columbia, Canada

Champions of Pleasure

Library and Archives Canada Cataloguing in Publication
Brame, Gloria G., 1955-, author
Champions of pleasure / by Gloria G. Brame – First edition.
Issued in print and electronic formats.
ISBN 978-1-77143-374-7 (pbk.).--ISBN 978-1-77143-375-4 (pdf)
Additional cataloguing data available from Library and Archives Canada

Artwork credit: Front cover artwork © Alex Iby @alexiby |
Unsplash.com; interior artwork credit: Handcuffs of love
© LostINtrancE | CanStockPhoto.com; back cover artwork
© Vek Labs @veklabs | Unsplash.com

Disclaimer: This is a work of fiction. All names, characters, organizations, architecture, events and incidents portrayed in this novel are products of the author's imagination or are used fictitiously. Any resemblance to actual events and persons, living or dead, is entirely coincidental.

Extreme care has been taken by the authors to ensure that all information presented in this book is accurate and up to date at the time of publishing. Neither the authors nor the publisher can be held responsible for any errors or omissions. Additionally, neither is any liability assumed for damages resulting from the use of the information contained herein.

Moons Grove Press is an imprint
of CCB Publishing: www.ccbpublishing.com

Moons Grove Press
British Columbia, Canada
www.moonsgrovepress.com

For my two constant stars, Will and Jen,

my two distant ones, Kristen and Peter,

and with gratitude to Lily.

⋛ Contents ⋚

I went into the brilliant night

and drank strong wine,

the way the champions of pleasure drink.

- Constantine P. Cavafy

❧ Chapter 1 ☙

BUTTER

She was frigid and stern and warm and soft. She was evil incarnate in enticing clothes. She was ice cold with a heart of gold. She was a beautiful creature and a sadistic beast.

Her breasts towered over him as Dane knelt, barely daring to breathe. Her aggressively wide hips were so close to his face her thighs nearly sucked him in. He melted with devotion and fell prostrate at her feet. She was everything to him.

"Lick my shoes," she ordered.

"Yes, Mastress," he fumbled, his lips swollen

with excitement. Something was wrong. His tongue was thick, frozen in his mouth. "Misbrest!" Fuck, why couldn't he pronounce the word right?

Was he having a waking dream or was he drunk with lust? He felt so weak inside, like his innards were melting. He suddenly remembered that she'd poured him a glass of thick black wine and he had drained it to the last bitter drop. Maybe she'd drugged him, like Circe. If that was her will, he was ready to turn into a pig for her, to follow her around all day and eat from her hand.

"Mistress!" the word finally escaped him like a sob. "I'm your slave!"

He couldn't see her face. His own words made him wild. She owned him, he was her helpless animal, her toy, her chattel. He would be anything she wanted him to be. There was no limit to what he would do to please her. There was nothing but his lust and devotion, no other reality, no other place he wanted to be.

He licked her perfect shoes, then removed them with trembling hands. His lips roved hungrily over her naked toes. His tongue dug into the sweet, humid clefts between them, tasting hints of creamy butter and fresh sea-salt. It was the taste of erotic adventure into the very fleshpot of life. This was the life he was born for, to know ecstasy at her feet.

He realized now that it was her sweat he'd imbibed, not wine. It was a magical potion. His transition from Dane to slave dane was complete, his thirst for her would never be quenched.

The more he worshipped her with his tongue, the warmer and softer her body became. He felt a tingle in his groin, then a tingle at the base of his spine as an electrical force surged into his pelvis. His testicles ached deeply. He needed to cum. He wanted to cum. He was born to cum groveling at her feet, like the animal he was. But he could not. Something was wrong.

The heat of his passion for her made him dizzy.

He felt like he was going to pass out. He grabbed her calves to steady himself, but they were slippery and moist and he slid back to the floor. When he stared up at her, her whole body was turning to goo. She was melting right before his eyes.

His Mistress was melting. Mistress... he couldn't remember her name! But she was melting. All of her was melting. Her hips were dripping a tsunami of butter. Pools of yellow grease spread onto the floor.

He struggled to roll away from the impending horror, but he was trapped like a fly in her butter glue. He tried to remember his safe word. Fuck, fuck, he couldn't remember his safe word. Did he even have one? He couldn't remember if they agreed to a safe word. Her hands had dripped off her arms. She couldn't release him without hands!

Wait. He remembered the safe word. Butter. It was butter. His safe word was butter. He was going to die.

"Dane, Dane," his roommate, Booker, was

shaking him. "Wake up, honey, or you'll swallow your tongue."

Dane jolted upright, his hair smashed into a lopsided triangle.

"What? What the fuck just happened to me?" Dane muttered.

"You almost swallowed your tongue?"

"I did? No, I didn't." Dane shook his head like a dog, "Brrrrbrbrlbrblr," he vibrated his lips.

"You know, if a person actually swallowed their tongue and shit it out, they'd rim themselves," Booker said.

"The fuck?" Dane vigorously rubbed his scalp. "What the fuck did you just say?"

"You had another nightmare. You were twisting and grimacing like you were in pain one minute and the next one you were saying, 'Butter, butter, butter.'"

"Stop fucking with me, Book," Dane said. No way had he said those words out loud. On the other hand, how else would Booker know? Goddammit. He was wide awake now. He had to forget that dream.

"Breakfast?" Booker asked.

"In bed?" Dane shot him a coy, flirty look. It would be nice if Booker served him for a change.

"Yeah... those looks don't work on me, grasshopper." Booker sat on the bed and folded his hands in his lap.

Dane sighed and stood up. "Yeah, yeah, I'm going."

Omelets were waiting in the oven, hot and fresh. Dane quickly assembled fruit and rolls to go with the eggs, and ground the freshly roasted coffee beans in the coffee maker. Dane had naturally eased into the roles of sous-chef, busboy, kitchen maid, toilet unclogger, bug killer, garbage disposer, heavy box lifter, and all around butler/ factotum for Booker.

He finally had the tray ready and was almost

through the bedroom door when he sloshed a cup. Damn. He stopped to slyly lick the tray clean again, then carried it into the room and set it on the bed.

They reclined facing each other, the way they always did, leaning on their left elbows and eating and scrolling their phones with their right hands.

Dane poked at the omelet with his fork.

"I used Brillat-Savarin. Did I tell you I got some at Zabar's?"

"Oh yah, yah," Dane lied. He stabbed the omelet and a greasy yellow drool oozed out. He closed his eyes and forked it into his mouth anyway. "It's good," he said.

"But not that good, right?" Booker inquired tensely, "Not $10 better than camembert good?"

"It's hard with cheese in egg. They meld so there's cheese in the egg and egg in the cheese.

Which is which? It's hard to tell. Cheese or egg? Egg or cheese?"

"Thank you, Gordon Ramsay."

"Why do you even ask me?"

"You're my man on the street! My real people test!"

"Could you hurt my feelings harder? I barely felt that."

They smirked at each other, their eyes merry. Then Booker got serious looking and leaned back.

"Would you like to talk about your dream, Dane? It might relax you to get it off your chest."

"No, it won't." He drained the rich dark coffee in his mug. Booker was the king of coffees. He could never enjoy any other kind of coffee. "You just want the gory details for your dream class."

"Oh no, not for dream class. Nightmares was last month, we're on waking dreams now.

Speaking of which..." Booker produced a joint. "Got time for wake and bake?"

"Nah, I got to get to the office early today."

Dane grabbed the dishes, ran them to the kitchen, put them in the dishwasher, then refilled his mug with coffee and sighed in contentment. He saw a spot on the counter, and scrubbed it until it gleamed again. He stood back and admired the expensive granite counters and state-of-the-art kitchen appliances. A good kitchen was a work of art. He was grateful for the beauty of their dwelling and its countless pleasures: the endless mugs of fine coffee, the endless spill of gourmet delights, the solid and tangible comforts of life with solid and tangible Book, a kind and generous human.

Their morning rituals together were simple and sweet. Just waking up and knowing he was safe and sound, ensconced in the security of a lasting friendship, made these mornings better than any mornings he'd ever known anywhere else. Life with Book literally made him happy every day.

If he could only get turned on by Book, it would complete their relationship, though, in other ways, it might put everything at risk. On one hand, both of them could stop looking for true love. They would be fully sufficient unto themselves. But in other ways, it would mean living a way he wasn't sure he wanted to live, or at least cutting off certain possibilities he'd always wanted. Like children. That wouldn't be impossible but it wouldn't be the way he'd always hoped it would be. He definitely needed a Mistress to serve. Theoretically possible, though a lot harder than he'd ever imagined.

From the first time they met, Dane knew that Booker would just never make him hard. Booker was gorgeous. He was too gorgeous. It was unnatural how pretty he was, like an anatomically correct doll designed by Disney. Booker wasn't just out of Dane's league, he was almost out of the human league. Aside from an irregular and oddly pale scar between his thumb and index finger from a skiing accident, there wasn't a pimple, a skin tag, or a wart on Booker's body to remind you that he was a regular person. Booker probably had a whole personal-care corps he visited on the down-low who squeezed, froze, snipped, lasered, sculpted, and injected him to perfection.

Dane wasn't bad looking. He had a naturally lean runner's body, although his belly was beginning to soften up from pizza and beer. His eyes were a deep royal blue that looked black in shadows. The perpetual farmer's tan of his youth had bleached out to Nordic white from years of city-life. His once platinum hair had turned a dark, dusty blonde in his 20s. From his chest to the tips of his toes, he was covered by light brown fur that hid all his freckles and flaws. He was only 28, but crows-feet and puppet-lines around his mouth were already getting etched into his face.

Booker had a decent cock, but it was long and skinny, as if all his exercises had sucked the fat out of it, making the skin too taut and the veins too prominent. Dane had a really nice one, and that counted for a lot. Dane had received compliments on it since his high school days, from women and men alike, so he felt pretty good about himself in that department. It was hardly the biggest one out there, but it had good length, good girth, and solid heft, enough to make people go "oooh" when they saw it.

It was always a high point for him when a Top ordered him to strip during a scene at a club and people gasped when the jeans flew off. He knew they wanted what he had, either inside them or instead of what they had, and he reveled in their lust and envy. If anyone cheered or applauded, he would take a blushing bow in their direction, which really got everyone going.

"You should talk a little about your dream." Booker walked into the kitchen, and pointed a vape pen at him. "Try some juice. It'll loosen you up fast."

"Nah, I gotta shower. You just want to analyze me with your psych buddies."

"I want to prevent butter trauma for life. I saw the way you looked at that omelet."

"What are you even talking about?"

"You stabbed that omelet like it was your dead mother."

"Oh, for fuck's sake." Dane snatched the pen out of Booker's hand. "Just one hit, then I'm showering."

"That's my Ding!"

"Ding fucking dong, dude," said Dane, taking a long hard pull on the vape.

Ding was what Booker called him because of all the dings he got at odd hours. As head of IT for ChicShoes, an Internet shoe warehouse, he was on call 24/7 in case of a site crash or whenever his team melted down, which typically happened at least three or four times a day on a good day.

"Why are you in such a hurry to get to the office? It's only 7:30. I was hoping you'd want to go to the gym and do weights with me. Something going on today?"

"Yah, we're starting the pre-holiday sales and I'm not 100% about the code. Plus, it's a club night. So I want to get out of there by 8 o'clock at the latest."

Just then, his phone dinged.

"It's like they own you," Booker said. "When, really, I own you."

Dane rolled his eyes. It was Margie from work. Instead of texting her, Dane grabbed the pen back and took another dramatically deep draw. He held his breath before accepting the call.

"Margie, hi, listen I woke up congested," he finally gasped the words out as smoke exploded from his throat, billowing into a thick cloud around him. He coughed until he thought his lungs would fall out. "Please don't cry, Margie, I'll be fine."

"Diabolical, Ding!" Booker was bent with laughter. Ding shushed him and walked to the sink for a glass of water.

"Yes, I'm taking some medicine right now.

Awww, thank you, but not, really not necessary, thank you for offering. I'll be there my usual time."

"Poor Margie," Booker said after Dane ended the call. "Poor lonely Margie."

"I know. She cried. I hate when that happens."

"Did she want to bring you hot soup and fluff your pillow?"

"Not funny," Dane said. "Yes."

"Not funny," Booker agreed, "just poignant."

"She's a doll," Dane said mournfully.

Booker once suggested that Dane should ask Margie out for a date, but that was a line Dane would never cross for personal and professional reasons. For one, his fiefdom of computer nerds were the most emo geeks he'd ever met. They brought all their raw emotions to work with them, something he was completely unprepared for when he first took the job, but soon he was sucked in so deeply he felt like he spent more time playing mother hen to 30 fuzz babies than to coding and quality control. He once walked in on a senior coder named Brett crying quietly at his computer screen.

"What's the matter, Brett?" Dane stepped up to him and put a hand on his shoulder. "Something at home? Do you need some personal time?"

"Look at this. Just look."

Dane saw a special sale on discontinued shoes. "Is something wrong with the sales price?"

"My father wore those exact shoes to his wedding." Brett enlarged the old-fashioned lace-up shoes. "I borrowed his pair to wear to prom, and 20 years later, my son borrowed a pair like that from me. And now nobody's son will ever wear shoes like that anymore."

Dane studied them. "They're pretty ugly, Brett. Maybe they deserve to die."

"It's just, you know," Brett breathed through his mouth, "everything's changing! Everything! It's not right. Why do things have to change? What do people even want from life anymore?"

Dane awkwardly patted him on the shoulder. "You've got to let go, Brett. The stress is bad for you." Brett heaved a sigh and his shoulders sank.

"What will my grandson wear to prom?"

"I don't know, Brett. Nike?"

"Fuck me," Brett said, trying to fathom it. "Nike."

Dane's compassion did not go unnoticed. His predecessor infamously monitored IT like the Gestapo, reporting the crew for eating at their desks, making them sign in and out on charts posted at every cubicle, even tracking how much time they spent in the bathroom. Dane became their superhero when he pulled all the charts down, told them they could snack at their desks and work through lunch if they needed to, and that, from that day forward, people could take the shit they needed to take, and not the one dictated by corporate bean-counters.

Their bond with the new boss had been cemented at their first department meeting with Dane.

"You would not have your jobs if we didn't believe that you are competent and responsible adults," he told them, "and since you are, it's disrespectful to treat you as if you're children in need of constant supervision."

After that, it was an alarmingly quick transition to Mother Hen and her hungry chicks. By acknowledging that they were strong and independent, he'd unwittingly given them permission to act weaker and more dependent around him. They even bobbed their heads in greeting and danced around a little when he passed, as if one sniff of his pheromones put them in a better mood.

They chirped out, "Hi, boss!" when he came through the door, and rushed over with random questions, like "Is it going to rain today?" as if he knew more than their weather apps. Sometimes it was more personal. "Did I wait too long to have sex with him?" or "Should

I go to that party where I could bump into my ex?" they'd ask, as if he knew a secret code to solving life's problems. His employees gave him far too much credit for knowing things. He was just a kinky code monkey with an Ivy League degree.

One Christmas night he left a party in Yonkers to ride all the way downtown on an SOS from work to find the whole department in chaos. One group stood helplessly around the server, arguing. Others were taking their computers apart. The table in the conference room was barely visible under a Sargasso Sea of cables and wires. Dane saw Brett hiding under his desk with an entire cake, carving slices with a plastic knife.

"What up, Brett?" Dane casually inquired.

"Shtressh," Brett said through a mouthful of cake, pointing towards the server station.

Dane walked to the server, while people rushed up to him and explained all the different fixes they'd tried. The crowd grew hushed when Dane stared at the server, stroking his chin in deep thought, squinting at it. The crew stood angrily at his side, clutching cans of compressed air and tiny screwdrivers, prepared to disassemble the beastly machine down to its mangy guts.

"Was the maid here tonight?" Dane asked. "Did anyone notice?"

They conferred loudly. "Uh, we think so." The question unnerved them. Was she the culprit? Maybe she was a corporate spy. Or a political malcontent who wanted to ruin Christmas for shoe-shoppers the world over!

Dane went to the wall behind the server and rolled his eyes. This wasn't the first time a maid unplugged vital equipment to use the outlet for her vacuum cleaner. He plugged the server cable back in.

"Yay!" one of the workers shouted. "It's coming back to life!"

"Yay!" several others joined in.

"We couldn't have done it without you!" a

woman cried and everyone starting laughing like it was all a good joke, patting him on the back and teasingly calling him their Savior.

After that episode, they somehow respected him even more, which he found funny and tragic at the same time.

Basically, his job and his people were a life-suck. He knew it. Booker knew it. Only the people who depended on him didn't know it. Weirdly, though, there were times he liked it. It made him feel so needed.

"Hey, you. Would you like to hug?" Booker lightly tapped his shoulder and brought him back to the moment. It was hard for Dane to stay in the moment. Memories and ancient scraps of conversations coursed through his mind as if they were still real.

"Hugs always welcome!" he threw his arms open to his friend.

After a lifetime of being starved for affection, Dane loved to fill up on hugs. No one had ever hugged him as much as Booker. It took a while to get comfortable with it, but Booker said it had genuine therapeutic value to hug and be hugged. As usual, his older friend was right. Now, if he didn't get at least one good hug from Booker every day, he felt a little disappointed. Booker taught him that hugging for no reason except mutual affirmation was the best reason to hug in the world.

Booker hugged him tight. When he let go, Dane stumbled. "I am ripped to shit," he whispered into Book's ear as he fell against him. Booker half-led, half-carried him to the sofa and pushed him down.

"I'll get you another cup of coffee. I'll make it extra strong."

"I love you," Dane said.

He let the high roll over him and surfed through his scattershot memories, his thoughts and his fantasies as they remixed in his mind. The dream. Lorraine. The office. And how he met his best friend, the incomparably classy, rich and intellectual Booker. Booker was the miracle in his life. Booker was the reason that he wasn't the same fucked up man he was before they met.

Speaking of which, the better Dane needed to get his shit together. He needed a shower. He glanced at his phone. 7 new messages, 3 from Margie, the rest from other concerned staff offering to run to the drugstore for him.

Their kindnesses still didn't compensate for the hellish day ahead. No wonder he had nightmares. A new sales program meant a lot of glitches, and a lot of glitches meant a lot of Pepto and Tums getting passed around the office. He couldn't stand going through another Sales-mageddon like they'd had last year, when shopping carts from Tulsa to Timbuktu failed. He'd installed new protocols and quality controls this year, but bugs were inevitable. Plus he had to get out by 8 pm, so he could talk to Lorraine when she arrived. She'd been acting really pissy the last few weeks. He had to see her and make some sense of what was happening with their relationship. But first, he really needed to reach some resolution on his job. Should he get out before it was too late or should he stay and tend to his flock? He should go. It was so obvious.

Booker handed him a steaming mug of coffee. "Thank you, thank you." He slurped.

"Coming down?"

"Starting to. The coffee will help. Actually, I made a big decision!"

"Oh, do tell!"

"I've made a decision about Lorraine."

Booker gasped. Dane himself was surprised by his statement and repeated it silently. He wanted to say he had decided about work. Even though it wasn't the decision he planned to make, now that he had said it out loud, he was on fire. YES! That was the decision! He was the dragon, and his words were flames! "It's time!"

"You're ending it with her?"

"No! I'm asking her to be my permanent Mistress."

Booker's jaw dropped. "I wasn't expecting that. So you're basically asking her to marry you?"

"Oh come on, you know that's not what it's about."

"Permanent is permanent."

"You know Mistress/slave relationships aren't about marriage."

"They're a kind of marriage." Booker repeated wonderingly, "We're marrying Lorraine. Wow."

Dane was too stoned not to be the sort of earnest he would wince to remember. "It's a deeper, realer bond than just having a legal document. Master/slave is about your authentic self. Marriage is just social permission to hook up." The power of his dragon mind soared to new heights of highness. "Those are the false heteronormative constructs we always talk about, right? BDSM subverts the constructs. It doesn't need or want institutions to agree." He was totally fired up now. "Fuck the institutions, am I right?"

"Drink your coffee," Booker said. "I don't think you've come down as much as you think you have."

Dane sulked. He still nurtured the fantasy that, somehow, through their mutual love of him, he could keep Booker and have Lorraine, too. "I know how you felt about Lorraine that time you met."

"I felt like calling Ghostbusters to get rid of her malevolent ectoplasm."

"You only met her that one time. ONE time!"

"But the way she priced everything, like she was casing the place," Booker said.

Dane defended her in his mind. That was a class thing. Booker never had to look for work or worry about his bills. He was born with a platinum spoon in his mouth. Lorraine was more like Dane, one of the "little people" who worked for people like Booker's father and made them richer. He understood her fascination with wealth. Booker's home was like a museum to people like he and Lorraine. That was why he'd brought her there. He wanted to share it with her.

True, Lorraine did not make the best first impression. She arrived two hours late and, okay, it was low-class how she kept asking Book what he paid for his furniture or how she kept eyeing an expensive crystal vase like she was wondering how it would look on her table.

Booker would never understand what it was like to hold down several part-time jobs just to make ends meet. Dane had to take a lot of jobs and cut a lot of corners to get food in his belly in his college years. He knew what it was like to feel financially insecure and to envy people who had all the money they ever needed. Money was power. Dane got it.

Besides, she was a Domina. It was only natural she'd want to have power. As a Domina, she had a right to be bitchy. That's what everyone loved about femdoms, that they were mean, selfish bitches. Booker wouldn't understand that because he saw everything through a non-kinky lens.

"OK, honey," Booker said. He was swiping something into his phone. "If you need to resolve the Lorraine thing I'm all for it."

He looked up from his cell and gazed sympathetically into Dane's eyes. "You know I support you and admire you for pushing all your sexual boundaries, for pushing yourself to try new things and how your BDSM keeps evolving. It's cool. I'm just a boring old homo. You are the new world. I appreciate it. I don't want to hold you back from exploring. I accept it."

"THANK YOU." Dane jumped up and hugged Booker hard. Now he was sober enough to get ready for work.

"OK, so the butter dream was about Lorraine." Dane confided. "She turned into a butter monster or something. UGH!"

"Butter MONSTER!" Booker said. "How felicitously Freudian!" He tapped on his cell.

"OMG are you Facebooking that?!"

Booker stuck the phone in his pocket. Facebook likes rang from his butt.

"Agh, fuck, whatever!" Dane went to the bathroom. "Have fun analyzing me."

Once the water temperature was perfect, he hopped in and floated away in sex fantasies. What if today was his last day on earth as an unowned submissive? Once Mistress Lorraine put her permanent collar on him, she would get to call all the shots.

The thought of it paralyzed him with lust. He'd do anything for her. It would be so friggin hot if she ordered him to marry her! He'd read posts from married subs who said their wives forced them to get them pregnant too, like stud horses. Maybe she'd make him cum in tubes and not even let him fuck her, just inject his sperm into her pussy while he was forced to wear a chastity device and watch. The idea of it drove him wild. He stroked himself, he stroked harder, he stroked faster, he stroked to ecstasy and more ecstasy and blind ecstasy... and OH, THANK YOU GOD, he felt truly cleansed when the passion rushed out of him.

He felt he could break the walls with his hands now. He was Super Slave, man of action, a risk-taker. Even if Lorraine rejected him, at least he had tried. But he wasn't going to fail. His life was going to change tonight. He knew it in his gut's gut. That's why he had the nightmare. His old life as a horny bottom was about to end. The dominant of his dreams was going to drown the old Dane's bullshit and the Dane who emerged from the hot butter tsunami would be a happier, prouder, stronger man for it.

He was the dragon! He wasn't going to be some old dude in a nursing home who regretted making all the safe choices. He was going to be an old guy with exciting memories of all the crazy things he'd done. He would never forget tonight. One way or another, he would never forget the night he asked Mistress Lorraine to be her permanently owned slave.

"I love you," he called out to Booker, as he

hurried to the front door to begin the journey ahead to his Mistress.

"Love you more," Booker called back. "Wait, are you wearing my new black leather jacket?"

"Is it okay? Love you mostest," Dane called.

There was a long pause. "Fine. But you seriously owe me more details about your dream. Butter in the title would get a lot of academic interest."

"You promised you wouldn't analyze me anymore!"

"Your butter could be my opus! My breakthrough," Booker called out in pretend dismay as Dane laughed and pulled the door shut on his happy bubble of happiness.

❧ Chapter 2 ☙

FISH

Dane jumped into a packed subway at 72nd Street. There was an empty seat next to a poorly dressed, disorganized-looking guy, so Dane sat down in it, put in his earbuds, and tuned up "Nature Sounds: Sonoma Thunder."

The best rides were when he got a window seat and could stare into the tunnel's darkness, as if the world behind him didn't exist. But at least he snagged a seat. He closed his eyes and escaped into his thoughts, ignoring the commuter crush. Long rides gave him time to take inventories of his life today and his life in the past. It particularly cheered him to compare his life before Booker with the life he had now. Every day brought new insights, new revelations, and new reasons to feel good about his friendship with Booker. Reliving their memories together was his favorite commuting hobby.

Booker's relaxed approach to life and voracious appetite for learning and growing had transformed life for Dane. Booker seemed to understand the keys to a happy life. He wasn't just book-smart, either. Booker was a thinker and a doer. When you were around him, he was not just intent on becoming the best person he could be, he wanted you to do the same for yourself -- to reach higher in life, to push yourself to new levels of self-understanding, to develop any talents you had, and generally to be as true to yourself as possible. Unless your true self was an asshole. Booker didn't like assholes.

But when Booker said, "I care about your happiness,' Dane knew he meant it. He wasn't mansplaining or bloviating, or telling him he had the answers to life. He just pushed Dane to do the things Dane really wanted to do instead of merely talking about doing them. He realized how much time he'd wasted in his life saying he'd do something he never did.

Booker got him to take that course on leather-working he longed to take, so he could make his own toys. Booker even gave him a beautiful set of fine leather-working tools when he signed up. Then Booker spent hours, night after night for months, testing him with Spanish language flash-cards for classes at Berlitz and helped with tuition too, fulfilling Dane's dream of being proficient in another language. Booker taught him to make perfect pancakes and flawless soufflés. And when he cried, who was there to hold him and comfort him? Dane's own parents never helped him that much.

He never thought he'd feel such a sense of home with another human being. He recalled the Dane he was the night he met Booker as a lost boy. Smart-ass and cute but lacking couth or taste. He was all swagger and no self-confidence. Any apartment, any neighborhood, any meal, and any fuckbuddy was good enough for him. He told himself it was all he needed. He called it freedom.

Dane "didn't do close." He was a lone wolf. He didn't want to depend on anyone and he didn't want anyone to depend on him. Dane saw himself as the poster child for "too many hard-ons and not enough opportunities." His sporadic sex life in college was mostly obliterated in his memory by the amount of booze and drugs he needed to have the sex in the first place. His worst experiences were waking up next to someone who wanted him to stay. Like, "I don't even know you, I just fucked you."

Sometimes his buddy Stella would show up in his dorm room late on a Saturday night when they had both failed to find hook-ups. He liked her but she'd push her way into his bed and would not leave until the next day. Stella knew exactly what she wanted to do with her life: she wanted to graduate, get married, and have babies, in that order, by the time she was 25. It was her mission.

Dane had no mission beyond getting good grades and getting a good job someplace cool, like San Francisco or New York City. He was too uptight to tell her about his fetishes and kink, much less about his burgeoning bi-curiosity. He didn't see her as long-term partner material. If he ever got married it would only be to a dominant girl, so he didn't see the point of revealing his secrets to Stella.

Then Stella found him in bed with her best friend's gay brother. His worst fears came true. She went on a viral campaign against him. She ended her tirade by calling him a "homo."

Apparently, Stella thought that every time he came, he made a little deposit in her marriage bank. He'd unwittingly made about five deposits with her. For Stella, that meant the next step was engagement. All of her friends agreed, including her best friend AND the same brother he'd had sex with. They all felt he'd made some kind of semen pact with Stella, or owed her something for fucking her when she showed up in his bed.

He blocked her and decided the friends who cut him off weren't friends in the first place, and fuck them all, they were all assholes. But he learned his lesson: future queer sex was strictly on the down-low and with strangers.

When he got to New York, his new policy was "fuck one, fuck all, just don't fuck anyone who's looking for a relationship." The Net gave him well-lubed passages to easy, in-and-out sex. The niche market of indifferent fuckers turned out to be beyond imagining in the City.

Big dick, medium dick, small dick, cut, raw, hairy, naturally smooth, shaved, tall, average, short, skinny, buff, fat, twinks, FILFs, silver foxes, handjobs, blowjobs, rim jobs, Daddies, bears, cubs, otters, pups, tops, bottoms, switches. There were thousands of men looking for a gay trick they could forget by the next day on the Big City boards. All of them at his fingertips!

He had one rule for men and one rule for women. He didn't want to get too close to men. He didn't trust them. The less he knew about their personal lives, the better. He wanted to go in, have fun and get out as soon as the deed was done. Unless they offered him free pizza. He remembered the taste of tomato sauce drowning the taste of a stranger's cum in his throat. Pizza tasted even better after blowjobs.

His rule for women was they had to pass his screening system. Every detail counted because he might be meeting his future wife. So she had to sound smart, not so much college-smart as life-smart. She had to post photos that were sexy enough for him to feel turned on, but not too X-rated because that looked cheap. She had to love Game of Thrones and hate Donald Trump. Spanking skills were optional but bondage, high-heeled shoes and foot-worship were required.

Once, after a hot scene at Pummels with his Leather tribe, Lorraine told him he should choose whether people thought he was straight or gay. That bothered him. A lot. Shades of Stella! He identified as pansexual at the club. So did Lorraine! But she said her ex-husband was bisexual, and she left him because she was afraid of getting AIDS or him leaving her for another man, so Dane never revisited the subject of bisexuality with her.

He wasn't sure if he needed to have that problematic talk with her. He was hoping that once he committed to a woman, his bisexual desires would decrease if not vanish. A dominant wife could take care of that. She could put him in chastity so he couldn't do anything without her permission. He knew that once he promised monogamy, he would never cheat, never.

Besides, he was a changed man. He didn't try to date all the women and suck all the cocks anymore. He had come to the cold realization that even when you slept with someone different every night, in the end they were all the same person - the person you didn't want to spend your life with.

A hand shook his shoulder and Dane pulled an earbud out. The storm in his ears confused his senses. He didn't realize the subway was sitting still between stations.

"What's happening?" Dane asked the owner of the hand.

"We stopped," the man next to him said. "I wanted to know if you're going to eat that donut."

As was his custom, Dane grabbed a donut and coffee from the corner store before getting on the train and was still holding them in his hands, unconsumed.

"Is it a Boston Cream?" The man eyed it hungrily.

"Yes. You want it?"

The man took it from his hand. "Thanks."

"You can have the coffee too."

"How do you take it?"

"Black."

"Good. Give it here."

Dane passed the tepid coffee and fresh donut over, casting him sidelong glances. How do people end up like this guy? His clothes were stained and disheveled, too thin for the crisp autumn day. His hair was a matted nest of grease and his moldy teeth were stained brown. Yet, he ate the donut with delicate manners and spoke like an educated person. For all Dane knew, he was a former Harvard professor or bank president. Who's to say how people end up the way they do? He could end up that way some day.

He pushed the buds back in his ears, and turned the volume up. He switched to Zen Music for work and tried to be still in his body, and focus on positive things.

Booker was his Zen. His refuge. His home. For the first time, he felt like a normal person, as entitled to peace and happiness as other people. He loved waking up and drawing back his thick curtains to see Upper Broadway, eternally bustling as streams of people walked the sidewalks, going in and out of stores, waiting on sidewalks, hurrying towards the

72nd Street subway entrance. On sunny days, he pulled the curtains back until his bed was drenched in warm rays and he'd sprawl naked on top of the blankets and bask in the light.

When Dane met Booker the first time, he thought he'd come to the wrong building. He walked about and down and around in confusion, then texted Booker to get the right address.

"You said 2019 Broadway?"

"Yes, it's the Ansonia. Do you know it?"

"No."

"The entrance has arches. You can't miss it."

Dane had seen the building from cabs. He thought it was a hotel. Now he stood under its tall, ornate arches, peeking through the massive street-level windows into a palatial lobby. It was like a city within a city in there. He self-consciously adjusted his clothes and smoothed his hair in his reflection in the giant window before going inside.

The vast marble floors and chandeliers made him feel like he was in a museum in Europe. The lounge had heavy, plush furniture. He dawdled, unsure if the concierge peering at him from behind the ornate station would let him pass.

Dane wasn't half as well-dressed as well as the concierge in his sharp, fancy uniform. He felt like the straw man standing before the Wizard of Oz and being judged. Dane always dressed down for one-nighters, jeans, a clean t-shirt and red Keds. A security guard appeared, glanced at him, nodded at the concierge, then vanished again. The concierge made a whispered call and waved impatiently at him, granting him entry. Dane walked through the lobby in pure amazement. This was the kind of place he dreamed of when he was a kid.

A quiet modern elevator swept him up to the 12th floor. He took his time walking to his destination. He'd never be back. He would never live in a place so grand. So he pretended he already lived there, that this was him coming home after a long day at the office, and that when he arrived, a tall, beautiful woman in leather would throw open the door and cry, "Surprise!" Or maybe, "Darling, your dinner is ready."

What kind of a rich person hooked up on Craigslist, for Christ's sake? He hesitated on the doorstep. Some kind of wealthy freak? A politician? A Mafia guy on the down low? It didn't take long to find out. No sooner did he ring the bell than the door yanked open.

"Hello!" his host greeted him. "Come in, come in."

The man who opened the door was so far out of his league that Dane hesitated. He looked to be in his 30s and as polished as a living Ken doll! What did someone who looked like a model want from someone like him? If Dane was that beautiful, he'd never have anything to do with himself.

But Booker ushered him into a palatial apartment acting happy to see him. Heavy furniture and thick rugs covered gleaming hardwood floors beneath a tall, vaulted ceiling. The walls were covered with bold paintings and primitive masks. Blue silk drapes were thrown open on breathtaking views of the Upper West Side. A bouquet of spicy and sweet smells steamed from the kitchen, making him salivate.

"Want a tour?" Booker passed him a lit blunt. Dane inhaled deeply, then had a small coughing fit. He was reeling, his eyes like plates.

"It's good, right?" Booker touched his arm lightly. "You ok?"

"I'm fine, I'm fine." Dane was embarrassed. He couldn't believe how stoned he got off the single hit. Holy fuck. It was some crazy high-grade pot he'd never tried before, and Booker was smoking it like it was Iowa ditch weed. He was total amateur hour compared to his sophisticated host. "Give me the tour."

He didn't usually want to see people's apartments because they were usually as depressing as his own hole. But this was different. This was like an adventure into the depths of American wealth.

As Booker led him through his home, Dane felt a deep shadow of sadness in his soul. He was already regretting that he'd have to leave this place. It was the most beautiful apartment he'd ever seen. Whoever built the Ansonia built it to delight the tenants, not just to make a buck. He tapped a wall. The stifling shithole he lived in was a cardboard box by comparison to the solid construction of this building.

Booker must have been reading his mind. "Did you know the walls are all soundproof here? Some of them are 3 feet thick."

Dane gaped. What a great dungeon it would make! You could scream for days and nobody would ever hear you.

"That's why so many composers and famous musicians have lived here."

Dane was taking mental notes. He wanted to fill his memory with everything he saw, just in case he did get really rich someday. Huge leather couch, check, only his would be black, not brown. Huge fucking television, check. He was tired of watching Netflix on his tablet, he needed one of those. Black stainless steel appliances in the kitchen and gleaming black tile backsplash and countertops. Fuck yes, check. Very fetishistic.

Then Booker led him to the master suite. Black bedding, check. Light-blocking window treatments, check. Big furry rug by the bed, check. Homo-erotic art above the headboard, nice, but his erotica would have a BDSM theme and women. Maybe a giant portrait of a femdom in black leather. He looked up. No mirror over the bed. OK, that was admittedly tacky. Check. Don't be tacky when you're rich. Check. The guest room was uninspired. Lots of floral fabrics. Zero checks.

"It's the only room I haven't redecorated yet," Booker explained. "We inherited this place from my aunt. She was a great lady." He looked wistful. "She was the greatest lady."

Dane tried not to tune in. It broke his rule to find out too much about a man. He focused on the house, marveling over every architectural detail and every painting on the wall. Everything was carefully chosen for display as if the whole place was one continuous work of art from living room to bathrooms, from warm wood floors to vaulted white ceilings. He marveled at the quality. Quality paint and quality paint jobs, quality floors installed by quality professionals, quality furniture from quality stores. He was a million miles from his little home town of Elkhart.

The living room ceiling fascinated him. He wished he could float up to look at all the details in the trim work. He wanted to touch it with his fingers. He wanted to fly up there back and forth, like a trapped bird. It would be intense to get suspended from a ceiling so high.

You could install winches on top. He imagined himself hanging from the towering vault. He imagined thick manila ropes hanging down from the winches, brushing the floor. He saw women in black boots securing him with bondage gloves and bondage boots and raising him slowly, foot by torturous foot, clear to the top, where he would fly and fly, and when he'd look down, the leather goddesses below would be watching him with cool, amused faces.

"OK, let's eat, handsome," Booker said, "or things will start to burn." He loped to the kitchen and began pulling pots and pans off the stainless steel stove, neatly arranging the food on fine white china.

Dane hadn't had a home-cooked meal since moving to New York. His plate was filled with treasures he couldn't afford at restaurants, from chanterelles sautéed with shallots, to slices of Kobe steak with a truffle reduction, and a side-serving of bone-in bacon that sent him over the top. Dessert was a small serving of kiwi sherbet and a mix of macadamia nuts and giant cashews.

Booker poured them both double shots of intense espresso that woke him from head to toe. It was the best dinner he'd ever eaten. Every bite was a blessing. He felt sad he'd never get to eat so well again. It was already the best dating experience of his life and they hadn't even gotten to the bedroom yet. It gave him a weird romantic feeling he'd never experienced with a man before.

As they ate, Booker asked him question after question. Maybe he put truth serum in Dane's food or maybe the food itself made him drunk. Or maybe it was the never-empty wineglass Booker tended like a sommelier. Oh yeah, the wine. Fine wines. An amazing Bordeaux and a fantastic Barolo. It made his head swim, but not with the sloppy haze of cheap wines. His head was swimming with clarity. New revelations. Enlightenment. Like he was being reborn as a happier, more satisfied, more sophisticated human being, as if the wine washed away the memories of his youth.

Conversation flowed so easily it was as if they were old friends. He'd never had such an intelligent and meaningful conversation before. He'd never felt such a sense of camaraderie and emotional equality. No one had ever seemed as interested in him, much less so amiable and friendly to him.

The conversation went deeper. Dane told Booker his whole life story, from angry mother and absentee father right up until the last time he saw his brother Tim. Booker nodded support and made empathic insights, and kept filling his wine glass. He reached across the table and squeezed Dane's hand.

The subjects grew broader. The energy in the room rose. The more they talked, the more little things they found in common.

They both loved music and hated watching sports on TV.

"Americans wouldn't be so fat if we actually did sports instead of watching them," they agreed with pursed lips. They complimented each other generously on their mutually fit physiques. Booker was a gym rat; Dane's years of running still showed. They bent over the food to lightly touch each other's hands and smiled lovingly.

They both loved museums and hated Broadway shows.

"Nobody just bursts into song in real life and has a chorus join them! That's ridiculous!"

They made each other crack up. That night, Dane laughed more than he'd ever laughed ever in his whole life.

He took stock of himself in Booker's bathroom. His eyes looked brighter. When he smiled, it didn't look forced. He was having a good time. Inside, his belly purred contentedly, all filled up with healthy food. He patted it happily.

Dane returned to the table. Booker looked so beautiful to him, his heart raced. He awkwardly sat down, spilling a water glass. He turned bright red.

"I'm sorry," he said. "I'll clean it up."

"No worries, the table needed watering."

Dane heard himself giggle and it felt strange. He was of taciturn Danish Midwestern stock. He wasn't an open book like some people who can be your best friend in five minutes. He had walls inside of his walls. He knew it. He liked it that way. It seemed like the safest and most appropriate way to be. Nobody needed to know what was inside someone else. But Booker was a master of breaking walls and Dane couldn't help but relax and reveal himself. It was new. It was weird. It cleansed him.

By the time desserts were done, Dane was a hundred years younger. "So that's how I ended up in New York, working for Big Brother's Little Brother, ChicShoes, and sharing a tiny shithole with three shit lords," he slapped his palm on the table. Cutlery clattered to the floor. "Oh, shit, I'm so sorry, shit."

"Don't worry about it, no problem," Booker said. "It adds a certain ambience to the room." He threw some of his own cutlery on the floor.

"Seriously?" Dane breathed, bemused.

"They're forking on the floor."

"You. Didn't."

"It's a forking orgy," Booker cackled, going to a cabinet to break out another bottle of wine.

Dane almost laughed out loud again when the train lurched violently, moving and then stopping with an agonized squeal of the brakes that jolted Dane out of his raucous memories. He landed against an old woman, who roughly shoved him back upright with a cold and bony hand.

"I'm so sorry," Dane was appalled. "What happened to the guy who was sitting here?"

"It's my seat now!" she said in a loud voice. "I got it fair and square!"

A nice looking older man holding a grab handle over them said, "He left. Can you believe it?" Dane could tell by his accent that he was a native New Yorker, and by his shoes that he worked on his feet all day. Store manager? Medical tech?

"Did we stop at a station?" Dane asked him.

The stranger got excited. "No, that's the thing. He eats your donut, he drinks your coffee, he puts the napkin and paper cup in his pocket, and then he gets up and opens the door, don't ask me how." He pointed to the normally locked door between cars. He nodded at the woman beside Dane, "The lady was shaky so I let her take the seat."

"My bursitis," the woman moaned.

"I seen him climb down the tracks like a monkey," the guy chuckled. "Noo fucking yawk."

"Oh my gawd." Dane covered his mouth. "I hope he's okay."

"He's a homeless bum," the woman snapped in disgust. "They're like rats. They live in sewers and ride for free. You'll see. He'll get to the station before we will." She looked angry about this, like he was using a bum privilege card to outwit paying commuters.

Dane and the man shared a look, then looked away. Dane wanted to defend his departed seat-mate's humanity, but he was tired of arguing with the heartless bitches who'd come out of the closet since Trump got elected. He put in his earbuds and turned on dark music so he could brood.

"All men are unequal," his biological brother Tim once told him. "There are winners and there are losers. Don't be a loser."

Wasn't it obvious the lady next to him thought she was a winner and the guy with tattered clothes a loser? She was just like Tim. If Booker was the light of his life, his biological brother, Tim was its abyss. Tim was almost 15 years older than him and bullied him from the day he was born. He resented sharing a room with Dane and took it out on him, yelling at Dane if he touched any of his things, making him look bad in front of their parents, picking fights so he had an excuse to beat Dane down and humiliate him.

Tim was no kind of a brother. Tim was never there to stop the tears or reassure him or stand up for him when Mother had one of her moods. The brothers never did normal brother things. They never saw a ballgame together. They never went fishing together. They never even had a good laugh together, not that Dane could remember.

The last time they saw each other was at his parents' funeral. It was the worst day of his life. His youthful dreams died that day. The dreams he cherished that one day they would be a happy family, that his mother would sober up and his father would love her again, and that he and Tim would bring their own children home for Christmas to adoring grandparents and a renovated farmhouse, all his rose-colored fantasies died with his parents. None of them would ever happen. He'd never hear his old man say he loved him. He'd never get his mother's approval.

Yet, he also felt an unaccountable surge of relief. He could go to college. He could lead his own life, free of their sordid control and rejection.

"I was not expecting you," his mother told him when he was a child. "If I knew then what I know now, I would have gotten an abortion." She actually said that. "You don't know what it's like to feel fat and bloated like a dead heifer and the doctors won't give you pills to help you sleep because of the baby. The baby this and the baby that, always the baby. What about the mother?"

She didn't know how hard it was to be her son, how hard it was to take all her criticism and still hold up his head at school. She didn't understand how it felt to go to bed every night not knowing if he'd still have a home. She was always threatening to leave the family, and his father came home so late at night, Dane was already in bed. Then the fighting started, usually over something small.

"You double-cunted, two-faced degenerate drunk," Dane's father would rant at his mother while Dane quivered in bed, listening to every syllable through the thin walls.

She'd scream back, "Twenty years of washing your stinking socks and sucking your dinky dick and for what?"

Dane tightly clutched his bear, Mr. Bingles, and wondered if he was the cause of all their bitter hatred. He blamed himself. If he hadn't been born, they wouldn't fight like this. They would have divorced and found people who loved them.

Tim was the son they wanted. He was the only son they wanted. His mother could never see a flaw in her golden child. The wall above the couch was a shrine to Tim's days as school quarterback for the Spartans, when he carried his high school team to a huge victory. Back then, Tim had thick blonde hair and a high, tight ass. By age 30, his looks were gone, his sparse hair was clipped down to a crew-cut, his gut bulged over his belt and his ass was as wide as the recliner he sat in to watch the NFL.

No matter. Tim did everything right. He did it exactly the way his parents expected him to do it.

"Girls always liked your brother," his mother would say, instead of admitting that he was a man-whore who couldn't keep his dick in his pants. "He appreciates a fine whiskey," she said about his notorious binges that landed him in the drunk tank. "Tim is so ambitious! Look how far he's come in life!" she'd gloat, ignoring the fact that for every dollar Tim earned he owed a dollar fifty to ex-wives, abandoned children, and the tax man.

Dane had ambitions, but his were not about leaving a long line of broken hearts behind him or cheating people out of their hard-earned money. He dreamed of starting an animal rescue or founding a company that would find the solution to clean energy.

His parents thought he was an impractical idiot who would never grow up. "You're not as mature as other boys your age," Mother told him when he was 17.

She firmly lodged her foot in his ass when he told her he wanted to go away to college. Mother said they couldn't afford to pay for "useless" applications, so he secretly applied to Cornell with the help of a sympathetic math teacher and used his savings to pay the fee. When he got an acceptance letter informing him he would receive a scholarship, he thought he'd hit the jackpot. A paid ride through one of the best schools in the country. It was the beginning of a brilliant career for him!

It's not like he expected his parents to sing his praises, but he thought they'd finally have to admit their younger son was a star too, in his own way.

"Mom, Dad," he announced over dinner one night, "I hope you'll be proud of me. I got a scholarship to Cornell. Isn't that amazing?"

"YOU?" Mother cried out. "Who'd give you a scholarship??"

"Cornell," he said. "I just said so. I applied for financial aid."

"I can't believe it. Are you sure they didn't make a mistake?"

"Of course they didn't. I was the school valedictorian! What did you think would happen after I graduated??"

"I thought you'd get a well-paying job like your brother. What do you need college for? Your dad and I never went and we turned out fine."

"I'm going. You can't stop me."

"We'll see about that. I bet the scholarship doesn't even cover bus fare to New York," she said shrewdly. "You'll have all kinds of expenses you can't afford. Books, clothes, rent. Does the scholarship cover all that?"

Dane struggled to answer. He already knew it didn't even cover all the tuition he would have to pay. His stomach knotted up so bad he felt like he was punched. "I'll get a job," he said. "I'll find a way."

"We can't give you a penny."

"I didn't ask you for anything," he said. "I just wanted you to be happy for me."

"You'll get a job right here in Elkhart, where you belong," Mother said.

"Dad?" Dane appealed to him. "You want me to go to college, don't you?"

"Your mother is your mother," Dad stared into thin air for a moment, then dropped his head back down. "It would be hard on the family if you left. We're not getting any younger."

"Are you guys kidding me? I got a scholarship to Cornell," he repeated as if they didn't understand what that meant to a boy like him.

"What about that girl you were dating, what's her name, little Miss Math Class? I thought she'd be knocked up by now for sure," Mother said.

"Euw. I'm not ready for kids! Also, we broke up six months ago!"

"See what I mean?" she nodded to her husband. "He isn't mature enough for college." She pointed her fork at Dane. "Eat the roast."

"I need to be excused." He stood up and knocked his chair over. His stomach was hurting so bad he needed to make an epic fart, and he was afraid that it would unleash a torrent of diarrhea. The big college talk he'd waited months to have ended with him galloping away from the table to poop and weep in the toilet over the unfairness of life.

Three days later, his parents were dead. They went out for drinks at their favorite bar one evening and veered off the road into a ravine on the way home. It took a jaws of life to pry them out of the vehicle and by then they were dead.

Dane was getting ready to report them missing when the doorbell rang. Two officers gave him the news and drove him to the morgue. Dane numbly identified them. They didn't look real. It was like someone was playing a horrible joke on him and had created plaster molds of his parents, all twisted and disfigured by impact. He couldn't believe it was really them. It was the most horrible thing he'd ever seen.

The burial crowd was scarce, just Dane and Tim, their pastor, his wife and their four young children in a sunny graveyard on a beautiful Autumn day, fire-colored leaves sticking to the children's bright jackets as they chased each other around. Neither brother had much to say about their parents, so the pastor did the necessary, a crane lowered the couple side by side into six feet holes, and they all left while the cemetery workers backfilled the holes with dirt.

When they got back to the farm, a party was in progress. It seemed like the whole church came out for the reception. Cheerful women and girls were serving cold salads and hot casseroles, families were eating, gossiping and laughing when they weren't yelling at the little kids tearing the place apart. Some men brought 6-packs and sat out back on folding chairs in a big semi-circle, shooting the shit. It was like a church picnic. He realized most of them didn't even know his parents. The pastor probably just told them to show up and bring food.

At one point, the pastor stood up before the crowd. Now he had plenty to say about Dane's parents, and how they were upstanding members of the congregation for 15 years and never missed an Easter Service in all that time, and how everyone should be happy for them because they were in Heaven now and would be forever happy. He finished by urging people to give money to the Church in their memory, and said it would make them smile down on them from Heaven.

"You believe this shit?" Tim had sidled up to him, whispering.

"No, but it's comforting anyway," Dane whispered back.

After the last guests finally left, Dane sank into the cushions of the living room couch and buried his face in Mother's favorite pillow. The barest trace of her favorite perfume, Chanel No. 5, lingered faintly, a fragrant ghost of her presence in the room. It was the one luxury Mother allowed herself. She applied a dab to each ear, each wrist, and the hollow of her throat every morning of her life, like a warrior applying the strong medicine of paint to do battle.

"Hey, Buddy, you okay? Get your face outta there, that couch must have toxic mold by now."

Dane sat up, his eyes molten with grief.

"I'm glad that shit show is over!" Tim announced. He picked a half-eaten Kringle off a plate, then popped it in his mouth. He caught sight of his brother's tears.

"Jeez, you fucking crying now? Man up, will you? We'll both come out ahead on this, Buddy. I got them to sign a big insurance policy last year, when I saw their money was getting shaky." Tim sampled an abandoned drink and gagged, then took a deep breath and drank it down.

"My name is Dane."

"I know your name," Tim said.

"Stop calling me Buddy."

"Wow." Tim whistled between his teeth. "I didn't realize this was hitting you so hard. I mean, Dad, he wasn't around much, and when he was, he was an a-hole, and mom was an angry drunk. They died before the bank seized the house. Maybe they did it on purpose. Maybe it was a blessing."

"So we should be happy we're orphans?" Dane said. "Is that what you're saying?"

"No!" Tim looked hurt, but Dane knew he was more upset he'd been exposed as the shitheel that he really was. "I feel bad about it, really bad. I'll miss them. I'm just saying it's not all bad for you and me."

"Uh-huh," Dane mumbled. He knew Tim was glad to get rid of their parents and add to his personal fortune with an insurance payout to help with back taxes and child support. They paused uncomfortably.

"Alright, I better be getting home." Tim went to the door. "I packed the car before the funeral, so I'm ready to hit the road." Dane didn't respond to him so Tim tried one last time. "I guess next time I see you will be at your wedding?" He tried to sound jovial.

"Then I guess you'll never see me again," Dane said.

"Listen, can you be serious for just one minute? You gotta stop living in your head, in fantasyland. It's time for you to act like a man, Dane. Mother and Dad, they're history now. We'll let the bank foreclose on the house to avoid taxes, so the insurance money is your ticket out of Elkhart. Go to Des Moines and open a little franchise, maybe auto parts, it's steady. Then find a nice girl and settle down, get a nice home, raise a few kids, that's real life. You'll be happy."

Dane groaned inwardly. Happy? Tim thought that kind of life would make him HAPPY?

"Thank you," he said, knowing his sarcasm would be lost on his brother. "I'll definitely think about it." He finished the thought in his head, "I'll definitely think about how little you know me."

After Tim left, Dane folded himself up like a fortune cookie on the sofa, overwhelmed by the enormity of his loss. He was truly all alone in the world now. He felt numb. He didn't just lose his parents, he'd lost his brother in the wreck too.

He hadn't trusted Tim since that time Mother washed Mr. Bingles when she was drunk. She fell asleep and by the time she finally retrieved the bear from the dryer, his shiny button eyes had melted into flat dull clots of black plastic. Dane was only seven and Mr. Bingles was his world. He cried and cried that she'd ruined him.

"Would it make you feel better if I bought him sunglasses and a cane?" she laughed. Then she told Tim the story, and he laughed even more, and never stopped taunting Dane about it. Tim didn't care how he felt. He never did. How could he? Tim didn't even know how he felt. About anything.

With Tim gone, Dane went out back to soak up all the good memories he could remember and say the words he wished he'd said to Tim. "The reason I live in my head is because it's the only place I feel safe." Tim wouldn't have understood that either.

He squatted down and stared out at the abandoned fields he'd once loved to explore. Weeds grew where there used to be crops, and the barn's roof was torn up by a tornado, leaving timbers ragged and dangerous. Out of the old barn's wreckage, a cat suddenly emerged, peeking through the dusty cobwebs before elegantly escaping them. It was a young tuxedo. The cat stretched its nimble white paws forward for a good stretch, then strode up to him purposefully.

"Who's a friendly cat?" Dane asked. The cat rubbed against him and purred loudly. "Is this where you live now? Where did you come from?"

The cat did a double take and stared at him in surprise. "Meow."

"You understand me," he said to the cat. "I lost everyone." He scratched its ears and the cat rubbed its cheek on his knee. "You understand, don't you, little fella. You lost your family too, didn't you?" It was such a sweet cat.

The lady next to him dug her sharp fingers into his arm. "We're moving and I can't get up!" she shouted at him. "Help me! I'm stuck!" Dane pulled out his earplugs.

"What happened? What's the matter?"

"I sat too long and I can't stand up," she whined. "It's my circulation."

Her legs must have gone to sleep. Dane supported her elbow to help her get to her feet. She took a wobbly step, then fell backwards onto Dane, landing awkwardly in his lap. For the first time, he realized she was wearing Chanel No. 5. He unthinkingly pushed her off with a wild vehemence that catapulted her forward into the crowd like an old lady bomb. Passengers jumped out of her way to let her through. He watched her go with a bitter taste in his mouth.

A guy in a cheap suit plopped heavily into the seat next to him. Perspiration glued his white shirt to his chest and the suit's armpits were soaked. Dane loved clean, natural sweat, but this guy smelled like he was fermented in a Chinese chemical factory. Dane felt a wave of nausea and dizziness. He needed to get some air or he'd pass out.

He stood up and worked his way through the crowd until he found an uncrowded door and pressed up against it to stare out as the black grimy walls of the tunnels flashed past. The glass felt cool on his forehead, and his heart stopped pounding. He still wasn't used to riding in a sardine can 100 feet under the ground.

He focused on Booker and drifted back to the first time they were together. He knew almost the minute they started kissing that something didn't feel quite right. Booker smelled almost antiseptically clean. Not a trace of sweat, none of the steamy, raw man-musk Dane adored. It was like Booker had massaged expensive cologne into his skin his whole life so that the skin smell was gone, replaced by a kind of mannish mintiness.

The death blow was when Booker started to tongue-kiss him. Dane's penis shrank as he gently detached from the kiss and suggested they move it to the bedroom.

Booker grabbed him by the hand like a schoolboy, and raced him down the hall and into his room. Dane lay flat on his belly, to conceal his lack of excitement. He propped himself up on his elbows and watched Booker, who was lighting candles and incense in dark corners like an artful magician, his face illuminated by the glow of each match he lit. The room filled with small fires and clouds of jasmine and lavender wafted around the bed.

Dane was getting turned on again watching him transform the room into a pleasure den. It almost felt like a dungeon now.

Booker got into bed. "You have such a beautiful face. All Nordic angles and planes." He traced a finger along Dane's brow.

"Yeah, I'm pale as a fish. I wish I looked more like you. Your skin is so exotic."

"My dad is black from Baltimore, and my mom's Jewish from Chicago." Booker said curtly. "What's exotic about that?"

Dane blushed. He hoped Booker didn't think he was racist. "I meant your skin is gorgeous. You're gorgeous, like a movie star." He sighed deeply with longing.

The men clutched each other with new passion. Dane let himself go and locked into a full-body embrace, letting Booker suck on his lips. Their legs twined like wrestlers, their muscles pressed together.

It was 40 seconds of the greatest ecstasy Dane had ever known. Then everything unraveled, every minor disappointment magnifying into disaster. When Booker sensuously massaged his buttocks, Dane thought it would lead up to a spanking. It didn't, it just went on and on and on until Dane pushed his hand away because it was starting to annoy him. When Booker whispered sweet nothings, Dane cringed inside. Lovey-dovey sweet stuff was a turn-off. He wanted Booker to call him a cock-hungry whore, not get all sappy. He could feel Booker growing impatient too. Dane started shrinking.

"Well, this isn't working, is it?" Booker rolled away from Dane and onto his back, staring at the ceiling. Dane peeked at him but couldn't read his expression. Was he angry? After the big build-up with food foreplay, he probably expected Dane at least to be grateful. Dane felt worthless. He was an ungrateful bastard. Why couldn't he get it up for the sweetest man he'd ever met? On the other hand, why did Booker lie in his ad?

"Why did your ad say you were into BDSM?" he said in a huffy voice.

"It didn't. It said I was kinky."

"OK, true, so what did you mean by kinky?"

"Sometimes I like to wear women's underwear. The old-fashioned kind, you know, girdles and big brassieres."

Dane felt like an idiot. "I guess I should have asked you to specify before coming over."

Booker put on his bathrobe. "Nobody's fault. Join me in the living room whenever you're ready. You can take a nap if you want. I need to put food and dishes away."

Dane was relieved when Booker left. He closed his eyes and thrashed around in the bed.

The pillows! They were so soft. Check! The bed was another CHECK. The sheets felt like an expensive shirt, the kind he'd tried on at Gucci's pretending he wanted to buy it. You could fit an orgy in the bed and nobody would fall off. The mattress was like a floating cushion. He sprawled and stretched his long legs. Within seconds he passed out, sleeping more deeply than he had in years.

He woke up to the smell of bacon. He felt fully rested. Was it morning? The room was still dark, but that could've been the thick drapes. He strained to hear a shower running or signs of life in the bathroom. He pulled on his clothes and walked back to the living room, touching the eggshell-colored walls in farewell as he went.

Booker had set small plates on the carved mahogany coffee table by the couch.

"Sex wasn't great," Booker greeted him casually. "I made us a snack from leftovers."

"Sorry, I passed out, so sorry."

"Did you enjoy your nap? You only slept for an hour."

"It was amazing, thank you, and thank you for letting me nap." He gulped hard and took a deep breath. "Look, I'm sorry about losing my erection."

"Where did you lose it?" Booker blinked. "Should I send out a search party?"

"Naww, ahhhh." Dane flushed from head to toe and avoided eye contact.

"Look, sweetie. I like men hard or soft or in between, I just like men, ok? That wasn't the problem." Booker hesitated for the right words. "You're hot and I'm hot but together, we're not..."

"We're not sexually compatible."

Booker smiled. "I crisped up the leftover bacon. We'll finish it with cheese and coffee."

Dane was blown away. The entire experience was fucking him up. Booker was so fucking nice. He bet Booker was one of those gays who hosted Sunday brunches and visited their biologicals with their spouses on holidays.

Dane quietly dug into the bacon. Who even ate bone-in-bacon? He'd read about it once in a restaurant review, but he didn't realize you could make it at home. The more he ate and the happier his mouth felt, the more ashamed he felt about his performance in bed.

He owed Booker something. The least he could've done was provide a rigid member. All he'd done since arriving at Booker's place was take, take, take. He was an asshole.

But it wasn't his fault. It's how he was made. He needed the threats of punishment, the rough touches, the sense of someone taking him down hard to a place where he felt he had no choice but to surrender. BDSM was his magical key. He shouldn't have to apologize for it, though he felt like maybe he should.

After several minutes of silence, Booker said, "There's something about you, Dane. You're different from all the men I've met. I hate to think I'll never see you again."

"Me too," Dane said, bowing his head. He already started to miss Booker, and his beautiful apartment, and his amazing food.

"We don't have to part," Booker said. "There is another possibility. I really need a man I can trust for this."

Dane's antennae raised. Uh-oh. He knew this was all too good to be true. Maybe Booker needed some money, maybe that was how he afforded his fancy digs, getting businessmen to kick him the cash for his luxurious lifestyle. What shitball of crapola was he in now? He would never get caught in someone's scam. He'd gotten an education on rip-offs on Reddit. Dane chewed his bacon faster so he could scram.

"Would you be interested in renting my guest room? House privileges, except for my bedroom and bathroom." He saw Dane's face. "Don't worry, I'll get rid of the granny stuff and get you new furniture."

This wasn't Iowa. There was a catch. Dane kept his eyes on his plate, refusing to look Booker in the eyes. "Thanks for the offer, but I doubt I can afford it." He gulped down his coffee and stood up. "I guess it's time for me to hit the..."

"Shut up and sit down."

Dane automatically dropped his ass back down.

"I don't need a rich friend. I need a loyal one, someone who won't steal my things or bring drama into my home."

"Okay." Dane was willing to listen. Was Booker offering to be his Sugar Daddy? How many times had he joked about wishing he had one? Did sexual compatibility matter in that kind of a relationship? Would he have to worship Booker's sweet smelling ass as part of the bargain?

Booker explained that his father was controlling with money. When Booker signed up for culinary school before finishing his dissertation in psychology, his father exploded. "I didn't pay for 10 years of graduate school so you could cook for people!"

"What does your old man do?" He tried to make his voice casual so Booker wouldn't know that his whole body was pounding with energy, conflicted feelings, and lust for the lifestyle that Booker lived.

"He's an investment banker," Booker said.

Dane lowered his voice. "Does he know you're gay?"

"I played Chiquita Banana in the 6th Grade Talent Contest. If he didn't know by then, he figured it out that night." Booker rolled his head back and laughed. "I was a damn good Chiquita too. Made the whole costume myself. Spent weeks on the headdress."

Dane gulped. "And what happened?"

"I won the contest, of course!"

"I meant with your father. Was he upset?"

"Daddy is good people. He just sees me as a risk to the family investment portfolio. Daddy is the son of a federal judge who was the son of a history professor who was the son of a minister whose own father was a janitor at the church where his son grew up to be preacher. Lots of writers and artists in the family, too. This was his eldest sister's place. Aunt Cora. She was a poet. And a painter. And so much more. She was like a mother to me." Booker placed his hand directly over his heart. "And now he wants to sell it. He thinks it's more practical for me to move to a one bedroom." He shook his head. "For me, it's more about family history than family money. Come, I want you to see something."

Dane followed his host to a door off the bedroom. Booker threw it open to reveal a long, narrow room lined with bookshelves 8 feet high. A woven Indian blanket graced the far wall above a thickly upholstered divan. "This was

Auntie's reading room. It's a work of art," he murmured, "isn't it?

Dane was speechless. It was a little world within a world, the room looking like an old used book store, the kind you want to live in.

"Auntie has a copy of every book that ever mentioned members of our family, going back to right before the Civil War. She has a collection of genealogical records on the family that have been waiting to be archived in some University library and signed first editions that Sotheby's contacted us about. But you can't put dollar figures on a family's history. Especially not a Black family's history. I've had too many epiphanies in this room to part with it! It's my history now."

Dane went up to a group of framed photos on a shelf. There were dozens of old photos in elegant frames. One was from the 1940s of a group of stern looking black men in stiff suits and long silk scarves standing outside a bank, and another was a 1970s photo of a huge family sitting around a Thanksgiving feast, all the younger people wearing disco-style outfits. Above the photos, a long series of trifold American flags were respectfully boxed and hung on the wall, the veterans' names inscribed on brass plaques.

Booker pointed to a gold frame on a side table. "That's me and Auntie the time she took me to see the Macy's Parade." A shyly smiling woman in her 30s stood on a sidewalk holding in her arms a serious little boy in a tiny gray suit and shiny black shoes. Next to it was another, older photo showing a beautiful white girl of 19 or 20 proudly holding the same boy as an infant. "That was Mother," Booker explained. "I don't remember her. She died when I was 1. Dad gave me that photo last year. Can you believe it, he kept it on his desk until last year?"

Dane was almost in tears. "How did she die?"

"Suicide. Post-partum depression. Maybe undiagnosed mental illness. We don't know." He paused. "She left a note saying dad and I were the only things that had made life worth living but she couldn't anymore."

Dane was speechless. Booker's family felt more real to him than his own. For him, home was just home-base, the place you kept your stuff until you moved to the next place. It wasn't HOME home, like you saw in Hallmark Channel movies, where mothers baked cookies and fathers lit grills, homes where people treasured photos of one another.

Booker didn't just have a home home, he had a history and memories, with roots of a kind that Dane's own restless family never established anywhere they went. Before Elkhart, it was Des Moines and before that it was Ames, all preceded by nondescript towns in Texas and Ohio.

"What would it cost to rent the room?" Dane was too curious not to ask even though it still seemed like a dubious proposition.

"Could you do $1,800?" Booker asked. "We own the place but maintenance is high, so that would help. That would include utilities and most meals if you want. I'm in cooking school, so there are always leftovers in the fridge that need to be eaten."

Dane did the math in his head. He'd actually come out ahead and be able to save money with a deal like this.

"That's all? Just $1,800?"

"It's enough to talk Dad down from his impulse to cash in on a strong market."

"That's a hell of an offer." It was too good to be true. It had to be. He was paying $1,400 a month to live in a rat-hole and he spent another grand just feeding himself.

"You're considering a yes?" Booker smiled.

Dane had never met anyone like Booker. He was candid and generous and affectionate. He was like a shining spirit in a dim world. Booker made Dane feel perfectly free to be the self he could never be around others. And now he was offering him the rental deal of a lifetime. The night was like a fairytale. It couldn't be real.

"Why me?" Dane blurted. "I mean... why are you offering this to me?"

"Why not you?" Booker's voice was mild and concerned, like a therapist.

"So, it's not about sex..."

Booker stopped him. "First, are you even gay? You're bisexual, right? Second, I like it romantic and you like it rough. Makes a difference."

"I am a BDSMer for sure," Dane said, "and... a bisexual bottom."

Booker nodded his head. It was the first time Dane had been able to say it out loud without fear. He already knew Booker would never hurt him. There was just something about the man.

"Ideally, I'd like to meet husband material. And my goal is to find a husband, so I don't think we could ever work out," Booker said.

"Uh. We hooked up on Craigslist. You're looking for a husband on Craigslist?!"

"I tried Farmers.com but they only come with cows." Booker raised an eyebrow but kept talking, "So... this is not a sexual proposition, my dear. It's a rental to allay my father's fear that I will grow up to be exactly as fiscally irresponsible as he raised me to be."

Booker leaned his chin on his palm, staring pensively at Dane. Dane spontaneously imitated him in fun. Booker smiled faintly and crossed his legs, so Dane did too. Booker grinned. Dane grinned. Then Dane jumped up, twirled and clumsily bowed. To his delight, Booker jumped up and mimicked his silly dance. Soon both men were springing and whirling, again and again, until Dane stumbled and Booker caught him.

"We play well together," Booker said. He guided Dane back to the couch and took a blunt out of an elegant carved box. "Another hit for the road?" He held it out and Dane accepted.

"Life is a majestic river of opportunity and change," Booker announced. "My grandpa told me that once." He repeated the words in a stentorian voice. "Life is a majestic river of opportunity and change."

"I love your laces." Dane was finding it hard to follow Booker's words. Booker had saved the best dope for last. Dane was so high he couldn't stop staring at Booker's shoelaces. Booker was wearing sneakers under his long silk robe, and the laces had sparkling white pom-poms that jumped around like pom-pom girls when Book's feet moved.

Booker continued, "Think of life as a river, Dane. OK? Imagine a vast river with twists and turns, flowing with life but also with debris. We can throw out our lines and nets, but we can't control what the current brings. One day there will be fish. The next there will be branches that tear the net apart. It's a metaphor."

"Like oysters," said Dane.

"What about oysters?" Booker asked. "What do you mean?"

"Sorry. The word just came to me. I don't know why."

"What's important is staying alert at all times and prepared to take action." Booker picked up the lecture where he'd left off, "Over time, you will refine your eye so you can recognize a good fish coming your way. You will hone your skills and become fully prepared to catch it. You only get one chance to catch it because the river never stops flowing and carrying things away."

"Did you read that in a book on fishing?"

"No, it's inscribed in the Book of Life." Booker rolled his eyes at him.

"I feel like a blobfish."

"What?"

"Though I think they are poisonous. Did I say blobfish? I think I meant blowfish."

Booker rocked back and forth with laughter. "How stoned are you, Dane?"

"Stoned enough to ask what kind of fish you think I am."

"You're a flounder," Booker said. "But the tastiest kind, Petrale sole."

Dane loudly agreed, "YASSS!" He was a floundering flounder. Slightly bitter, but flavorful.

"I'm getting you a cab. What's your last name, by the way?"

"Jenson." Dane got his wallet out and showed him his license. "You might as well be sure, right?"

"Thank you," Booker said, memorizing the info and saying Dane's birthday out loud. "Useful." He smiled.

"And you?"

"Dodson," Booker said. "Booker Owen Dodson." He hugged Dane. "If you decide yes, you can move in anytime you want, tomorrow, next week or the first of next month, but no longer than that, okay?" His phone pinged. "The cab's here." He kissed Dane and pushed him out the door. "Text me when you get home."

Dane had no memory of getting on the elevator or how he got down to the sidewalk. He only remembered his joy. He'd won the lottery of life! He was moving into a castle where he would sleep in luxury and wake up safe with someone who really liked him and understood him and fed him gourmet meals! He swooned over the new life awaiting him.

A few minutes later, he was fuming with rage. He hated where he lived. He fucking hated it and he hated himself for living there. He'd fallen for the real estate ad like a pathetic hayseed. "Tiny Living in the Big Apple." It seemed charming until he got there. It was 800 square feet of hell inhabited by 4 men willing to sacrifice comfort for the convenience of living close to work in an elevator building. Amenities included listening to roommates wanking, moaning, farting and snoring. On humid summer nights, years of dried cum rose to life as redolent trails of heat-seeking bacteria that climbed inside his nostrils.

He'd pretended it didn't matter. He'd swallowed the shit. Now he couldn't stand to live there another day. He remembered Booker's fishing story. Booker was the fish worth catching. Until that moment, all Dane had ever caught in his net was debris. He hastily texted Booker from the cab.

"Can I move in tomorrow?"

He counted the seconds out loud until Booker texted him back and then how his heart soared.

"OMG. YES. Bring 1 month's rent, deposit not required."

It was so simple and easy and beautiful. It was the best day of his life. Whenever he got stressed he relived it in his mind. He just hoped Lorraine wouldn't try to come between him and Booker.

The subway was pulling into his station. It was time for his other life to begin and his inner life to go back in its box.

ᘒ Chapter 3 ᘓ

EVEN MASOCHISTS FEEL PAIN

Work was work. If it was fun, everyone would want to do it. He understood the system. You play to get paid. You invest a piece of your life and, in return, you got a paycheck for your effort. That's what middle-class life was all about. Some people treated it as if it was a big sacrifice to labor for a paycheck. To him, it was a fair trade: you give them intangibles, like effort, loyalty, and skill and in return they give you the almighty god of tangibility -- hard cash.

So, sure, a pointless morning meeting for department heads, but in addition to a paycheck there was a breakfast buffet and company gossip. A couple of hours of email, paper shuffling, phone calls and bullshit, but then his daily department meeting where they played games to build morale. Next were the phone calls with marketing executives and bean-counters, and then it was time to eat last night's leftovers in the company cafeteria.

When available, he took the small table between a pillar and the coffee station. It gave him the perfect vantage to people-watch. He'd subtly watch groups of women as they carried trays of food so close to their chests it looked like they were serving their breasts with the food. He loved that. He imagined them in corsets and sexy leather outfits.

The human dramas in the cafeteria were more interesting than reading a novel. He was fascinated by the people who acted surprised that they had to pay for lunch. Again. The way they did the day before and the day before that. Their attitude mystified him. Did they need the money for something else or did they really forget that food costs money? Some of them acted as if paying for their own food was a tedious imposition on their busy schedule.

The cafeteria workers endured their jobs patiently. He didn't look down on them. Maybe they didn't know it because he wore a nice suit, but he was actually one of them -- the class of people who take orders, clean tables and serve others in some capacity. Without the life insurance, he might have ended up wearing a uniform to work, maybe for a delivery service or the post office or something like that. He wondered if wearing a uniform gave people more or less incentive to do their best.

He had a regular trick who had a fetish for uniforms and collected them for every occasion and sexual predilection. His home was like a costume shop. You had to weave a path through all the haphazardly arranged dressers and rolling coat racks from which his collections spilled. Dane didn't share the fetish, though he thought it was incredibly cool and dressed up when the guy asked him to, once choosing a tight Navy uniform which reminded him of a Tom of Finland drawing.

In a way, everybody wore uniforms and masks in the world, everyone hid their real selves. Nobody wore their work clothes to sit on the sofa and watch TV. He bet billionaires walked around in their shorts and sweats when they got home. He wondered what Warren Buffet looked like at home. Probably like any other saggy-chested, pasty old white dude in boxer shorts.

It was all about context and knowing where it was okay to let the mask down and be your real self. Like, in a BDSM club you can be naked on all fours, wearing a collar, and nobody thinks any less of you. But if you did that on the street, they might call you insane and arrest the person holding your leash. Same if you wore flippers and a breathing tube to bed. That would be labeled perverted, but if you wore the exact same outfit to jump into the ocean, that was wholesome. Why? Who made up these rules?

BDSM opened questions he never even thought about before and helped him unravel the mysteries of social interactions in the world. He was especially fascinated with power dynamics and how people share power or impose power or give their power away. He knew from personal experience that some people just hand their power over to someone based on whether they wear the right clothes or have a fancy title. It was like once they saw the expensive suit or heard someone was a vice president, they shut off their critical thinking skills.

As he saw it, most of the management were Apprentice Dominants who supervised the labor slaves for their corporate overlords, the Company President and the Board of Directors. The big bosses held all the real power. They put freezes on workers' raises, paid men more than women, and issued pink slips without mercy. He knew the day he saw the work contract, with its morals clauses, that he was consenting to a totalitarian system. Unlike a BDSM contract, there was no room for negotiation. It was the Company's way or the unemployment highway.

He figured it out when he was a student, trying to decide on whether or not to take a corporate job. Work was an impersonal transactional power relationship. Your job was to produce for them and to maintain your value for as long as possible. If you were ambitious, you tried to increase your value to them by constantly developing your skills and climbing up the ladder as far as you could get. Then, you got old and your market value dropped. Either you retired or they fired you. It was a shit system, but it was the best way a boy like him, with no wealthy contacts or family money, could get ahead in life.

After lunch, he returned to his private office, watching his crew filter back in through his open blinds. He reluctantly loved his staff. Reluctantly because he was afraid of getting stuck at his job. The closer he felt to them the harder it would be to leave and he knew he would have to leave one day to make the kind of money he needed to start a family in New York.

They were a tight crew nonetheless. They

celebrated every birthday, and some of them exchanged holiday gifts. His office was lined with kitschy little mementos from their vacations, and he let them post pictures of their children and their pets on a brag wall outside his door.

Everyone kept things professional but there were hints they weren't totally straight. One of them was a lesbian and another was completely out as transgender. He saw occasional flashes of sex sites and chats on their devices, and overheard random bits of conversation that made him think some of them had something going on privately. Brent, who looked and acted like every Dad cliché in a sitcom, made so many jokes about swinging and threesomes that everyone in the office was mystified about whether he was inviting them home or just kidding.

Then there was Margie. Poor submissive Margie. His Kinkdar pinged every time she volunteered to ease his load.

"May I please help you in some way?" she'd ask

in a soft, whispery voice, looking up at him like a little birdie with big brown eyes.

She was such a sweetie! He could feel it in his bones that she craved to be topped. He didn't mind switching sometimes, but it was a line he could not cross with Margie. He would never sleep with a co-worker. He could never risk anyone at work finding out he was a pervert, even if they were queer, too. Margie's neediness gave her a Stella vibe. SAFE WORD.

He wondered how he'd feel if, one day, Margie showed up at a club where he was partying. What if he met her when he was naked, hands cuffed behind him, being led on a leash by Mistress Lorraine? That would be too much. What if Margie was the one who was naked, with a dominant leading her on a leash? That scenario didn't bother him one bit. Actually, that might be cool.

Dane checked the time. He couldn't wait to get to the club. He loved being around his own kind when they were someplace they could be free to be their true selves. BDSM people made sense to him. He liked the way they thought, he enjoyed the things they enjoyed. He felt an instant kinship with them from the start.

He had a handful of kinky partners in college, but in The Big Apple, he became an official member of the greater kinky-verse, a world of clubs and parties, community events and play-dates.

BDSM wasn't what outsiders thought. He knew because he was an outsider when he started. At the time, he thought being submissive meant you had no choice. You were just a lackey, a helpless piece of meat for the dominant to use. That's how it was portrayed in the jerk off books he'd read. But it was the opposite. BDSM was about making a complicated set of choices -- the role you'll play, the limits you'll set, the toys you'll use, the outfit you'll wear, the words you'll say. BDSM presented endless streams of variables and paradoxes to sort through. It was a phenomenally complex but also logical system. It appealed to him down to his bones.

Like, he wanted to be owned, BUT only by his

own free choice on who would own him and how she'd treat him. Or, he loved pain BUT he also hated it. And then there was the basic BDSM paradox that you feel pleasure from things that non-kinky people thought were sick and bad.

He loved kissing a Femdom's boots. It was not degrading, it was spiritual. It elevated his soul to pay humble tribute to a glorious woman's power over him. Spankings and whippings looked cruel only to people who feared pain. Sometimes pain felt emotionally good, even when it felt physically bad. The more he suffered for a woman, the more noble he felt, the stronger he felt, and the more he deserved respect. Pain was a ritual of atonement that healed something dark in his soul. The endorphins alone put him in a trance of contentment that could last for hours and leave him floating for days.

It was a rush to ask for and get the experiences he craved, to find his trance-space, his lust-space, and his love-space united when he did BDSM. He loved when Femdoms set rules, too.

You felt like all you had to do was obey and everything would be fine, the Domina took care of everything, you just had to obey. It made the world seem so simple and easy to be able to give up control and trust that Mistress knew best.

Lorraine had a rule that if she was talking to her friends, he had to wait on his knees until she granted him permission to talk to her. Then, and only then, would she acknowledge him. The rule reminded him that he was her slave, her property, there only to do her bidding and render her service. It made him melt to his core. It made him feel so submissive that it didn't even feel like a rule, just the fair terms for enjoying the attention of this goddess.

You couldn't explain that to a non-BDSM person. Booker admitted he was a little squicked by the idea of kneeling before someone. Or maybe Book was squicked because that someone was Lorraine. Dane wasn't sure.

Dane couldn't wait to get to the club. He

couldn't wait to see Lorraine. Every minute that ticked by separated him from the passion, the jubilance of giving his deepest self to HER.

Dane checked the clock and went back to work but his brain was overloaded. He couldn't handle the stack of emails sitting in his mailbox, so he focused on rechecking code until his eyes throbbed and burned.

Finally, he saw his day crew was packing up, while the night crew was filtering in. He had time to relax for 20 minutes so he grabbed his coffee thermos, walked to the elevator and rode up to a deserted employees' lounge a few flights up. Away from his office, he could sip his coffee while surfing his favorite malesub chat room, msubserv.

Last time he visited, the room was lit. Everyone was talking about Mistress Marmalade, a Pro-Dom on Long Island. Dane followed her story with an amused horror. A couple of months ago, a subbie guy accused her of being a rip-off artist, claiming he had proof she stole from him and other male submissives. At first, his message was flamed and shredded by her defenders, who claimed this was a betrayal of "a wonderful dear lady and long-time Community member who never missed a Divas of Deviance Ball in 5 years." It reminded Dane of the pastor's speech about his parents not missing Easter Services, which made him laugh.

A few more members came forward to say she wasn't as ethical as she pretended to be. After that, full-scale war broke out on the message boards between defenders and accusers. The few people who urged moderation got hate-bombed by both sides.

Dane lurked and devoured the controversy until the moderator banned a handful of vicious subs whose frustration had transgressed to threats of outing people. The moderator begged them to stop and warned them that the cops could be watching, they had no way of knowing. The second he read that, Dane logged out of the site and cleared his browsing history. He didn't want to get caught up in any of that. He avoided msubserv till things died down.

Now it looked like all the Marmalade threads had been scrubbed, replaced by an admin's post which provided links to FetLife, Facebook and Reddit. He settled comfortably into his chair, determined to follow every bizarre bend in this kinky tale for the next 20 minutes so he could be up-to-date when he got to the club.

He steeled himself for the shitshow of all social media shitshows. He was not disappointed. Marmalade, aka, Loretta was accused of scamming over $180K from clients. He clenched his teeth. This made the Community look really bad! People would think BDSMers were criminals and low-lifes.

A band of Marmalade's supporters who used @SweetJam on Twitter had set up a GoFundMe to raise money for her legal defense. They claimed it was all a politically-motivated witch hunt against BDSMers. A band of anti-Marmalade justice warriors who went by @PoisonJam on Twitter started a subgroup on Reddit, where they told people to boycott the fund drive. Both sides made good arguments. He didn't know who to believe.

It turned out that her landlord reported her. The men who got scammed were too spooked to call the cops and give their names. Instead, one of them tracked down the landlord, a Mr. Saxon, and called him anonymously. The caller told Saxon that Marmalade was abusing men at a sex dungeon in his rental property and that she was contaminating his property with depravity and crime. Apparently, Saxon had been waiting his entire life to report a pervert. He drove to the cops to report her and got their attention when he told them she had moved in with two children. Two children he hadn't seen in a couple of years. From there, Saxon began spinning insinuations of child endangerment and human slavery.

The cops called other cops, and they called other cops and social services departments. A week later, a small army of police, Federal agents, Homeland Security cops, and a child psychologist showed up on Marmalade's doorstep with automatic weapons, drug-sniffing dogs, and search warrants. Dane was aghast. He jumped to a Long Island news site for more details.

The spectacle of a woman who baked cookies by day and beat ass by night had stoked a media frenzy. In Long Island, where she lived as Loretta Lanzetti, aka, "The Cookie Lady," she was renowned for the home-style Italian cookies she donated to local events. In 2015, she received a business award for opening "Cookie Lust" at the local mall. This particular detail tickled Dane. It was so inappropriate for a cookie business, unless she made penis cakes or boob cupcakes. What was she thinking? He imagined a small child seeing the sign and looking up at his father, asking, "What's wust, daddy?" He shook with laughter.

Dane needed to see the video. He went to YouTube and watched stone-faced men carrying out boxes of BDSM toys and DVDs, then electronic and video equipment. A bondage cage and a cross were paraded next, hoisted high on blue shoulders. The men carried their weight as solemnly as pallbearers.

Another video showed Marmalade being taken in handcuffs. Talk about non-consensual bondage. They didn't even let her fix her hair.

She wore a tattered Betty Boop robe that trailed on the ground as police dragged her trembling like one of the dogs in those ASPCA ads he couldn't bear to watch. Maybe it was good for people to see her as vulnerable and scared. Maybe it'd make her more human, more identifiable to straights. But a part of him wished she was in leather, chin held high, dignified and proud.

Though her face was a bit blurry, there was something familiar about her. Maybe he'd run into her once at Pummels? He was sure he'd seen her somewhere. He was glad he avoided pros. Not that there was anything wrong with them. Still, you never knew if there were angry former clients or shady dealings going on until they snuck up and bit you on the ass. He had often imagined what would happen if he was ever outed. He'd lose his job for sure.

In another video, an eager young podcaster galloped across the lawn to interview a glum couple who were standing on the porch of the house next door. Desperate for moral outrage to spike his numbers, he affected a tragic expression before thrusting his mic in the woman's face.

"How did you feel when you found out the Cookie Lady was a dominatrix? You must be outraged," he goaded her. "Mrs......?"

"Giannini. Well, we're upset!" she said. "There go the free Sprinkle Cookies and the Black and Whites at Senior Bingo."

"I'm sorry, I don't quite..." the reporter was flustered.

Mr. Giannini came up behind her, crusty and irritated. "You know how hard it is to find authentic Italian cookies these days?" He grabbed the mike and shouted into it, "If you ask me, that's a bigger crime!"

"But what about the children!" the reporter spluttered. "Aren't you concerned they were exposed to depravity?"

"Children?" the old couple asked each other. "Her kids are older than you," Mrs. Giannini finally laughed. "They don't live here anymore."

"Our poodle is older than you," Mr. Giannini chimed in.

There was a brisk rap on the door. Dane hastily shut his phone off and slid it into a pocket just as the door nudged open.

"Sorry to do this to you, Dane, but we'll be shooting in here tonight." It was Lincoln, the company's Creative Director, and one of the only men at ChicShoes who was openly gay. He was pushing a big cart of shoe boxes. "We'll need this room until 8."

Dane looked at the time. "Oh, no, I didn't realize I'd stayed this long! Jeez, yeah, I'll get out of your way."

Lincoln pushed the cart into the lounge and Dane helped him wrangle it past the table.

"Feel free to grab a pair when we're done."

"Thanks, Link, your timing is perfect. I'm seeing my friend tonight."

"You must be getting serious," Lincoln winked.

"That's six pairs in the last four months."

"Noooo! You counted?"

"Not intentionally. I just have a good head for inventory. Especially the kind that disappears." He smiled. "Don't worry, all the executives hit me up for shoes. High heels aren't just for ladies anymore."

"Really!?" Dane wondered which of his stuffy senior colleagues slipped into stilettos at home, and which of them had boyfriends who liked to wear them. The whole world was queerer than anyone would admit!

Dane hurried back to his office. It was too late to order food from any of the good places. He ordered a burger from the crappy deli down the block, checked in with the night people, and spent the next two hours running tests. At 8pm, he combed his hair and packed up his devices.

He went back to Creative. The models were already leaving, but Lincoln waved at him and pointed to piles of shoes scattered on tables and floors. Dane picked through for something in Lorraine's size. He was about to give up when he spotted a pair of spike-heeled patent-leather ankle boots with petite gold buckles. They were in her size. He imagined kneeling at her feet and fastening them for her. Perfect! He popped the boots into his backpack and headed cheerfully to the elevator.

The only other passenger was a man in his 60s with manicured silver hair and dyed brown eyebrows and goatee. Probably an exec from another floor. He wore an electric-blue jogging outfit and an orange headband and stared straight ahead. It was impossible not to stare at his furry legs and shiny blue nylon shorts. He had a firm ass for a man his age. Dane could make out the faint traces of a jock strap and looked away before he got a boner.

The man took off at a run when the doors opened. He made a big circle in the lobby and ran right back to the elevator bank, jumping into a car going up. Dane was confused until he got to the front doors. Rain pissed down on the sidewalks and sewers were getting backed up.

His plan was to make a quick stop for flowers and still get to the club before Lorraine and her entourage made their entrance. He planned to be on his knees, head bowed, holding the bouquet of flowers in his arms, when she arrived. He wanted it to be a night neither of them would ever forget.

He stepped out onto the sidewalk and looked up. A wall of angry clouds clustered in the sky above. The street was empty and black. Cabs with passengers zipped by and a few limos waited in darkness for the moguls who commanded them. He ran from corner to corner in search of a cab, then texted Uber and Lyft to no avail. The club was too long a walk from work, especially in this rain. His shirt was already soaked, and he was worried that his backpack's waterproof lining wouldn't stand up to the drenching rain. At least Lorraine's shoes and Booker's jacket were safely tucked in the bag. He couldn't take the risk of getting them wet.

A cab stopped a few feet from the sidewalk to let someone off. As the door swung open, the cabbie shut off his availability light. Dane snatched the door handle as the passenger emerged umbrella first, and narrowly avoided getting stabbed in the eye.

"Going out of service, Sir," a tired voice said. "No more riders tonight."

"Please. I'll pay extra. I'll give you an extra $20, what do you say?"

"Let go of the door, Sir," the cabbie said.

Dane peered through the rain-blurred window into the front seat. The driver's ID said Max Schwartz.

"Please, Max." Dane pulled a $50 from his wallet and held it up.

"I'll make it $50." He thrusted it into the car at the driver, then hesitated when Max snatched it. Dane instinctively tried to tug it back from the cabbie's grip. "Will you take me?"

He looked up at the sky again. Was it really worth an extra $50?

A raindrop the size of a pigeon turd fell into his eye, nearly blinding him. He shrieked and stumbled off the curb, losing his grip on the money.

Max grabbed the bill and put it in the moneybag on the front seat, while Dane held tight with both hands to the door handle as a growing pond of ordure swelled underfoot, making him queasy. He loved walking in the rain in Iowa, bathing in the clear showers that fell from its wide open skies. He'd walked barefoot through pastures of cow and horse plop without care. But the idea of the piss and puke and ashes and sweat and blood and shit, 400 years of New York history pooling around his feet made him so nauseous he suddenly lost his grip.

"Fuck, fuck, fuck, no fucking way fuck," he shouted as he fell. He sat in a putrid puddle. The crack of his ass was squishy slimy, his socks were glue.

"Fuck my life." He checked his backpack. It was miraculously dry.

Max watched Dane's dilemma without blinking. "Holy shit, alright, get in before a raindrop kills you."

"I can't go like this, with a wet stinking butt. I have to go back upstairs and change clothes."

"Alrighty then, bye-bye," Max said. "Thanks for the tip!"

"Oh, God, no, please," Dane implored, "please wait for me! I might not find another cab for hours! Please. I'll give you another $50, I promise. Just wait for me."

"You got 10 minutes, can you do it in 10 minutes?"

"I can! I will!" The seat of his pants was as soaked and sloshy as a full diaper. He walked back to his office, making ass-music with every step. The night crew was too busy to pay attention so he slid into his office, locked the door, closed his blinds, and unlocked his credenza.

In there, he kept a few random things he was too embarrassed for anyone to know about -- Mr. Bingles vacuum-packed in plastic, a stash of Iowa Smokehouse jerky, a flutophone. He also kept a complete ensemble of emergency business clothes in case something tore or got stained during the day. He kept emergency clubwear in there too, in case he got invited last-minute to a party. He had a black leather jockstrap, a studded pleather chest harness, a black t-shirt, a pewter triskele pendant, a leather flag bandana, a pair of mesh underwear, and black spandex leggings, all of which could be mixed and matched and worn under a suit until he got to the club.

He pulled out the mesh undies and the pendant and crawled under his desk, then stripped off his wet clothes and got into the fetish undies. They instantly perked him up. He would always remember them as the undies he wore the night he pledged to be Lorraine's slave, to tie up and to spank forever more. He jumped into his emergency business apparel and rode down to the lobby adjusting his tie.

He tapped his Fitbit: he'd made it back in 11 minutes. He stepped outside and inhaled. The air smelled sweet and the rain had slowed to a misty drizzle. Max was nowhere in sight. Dammit. He peered into the thick fog. It was no use. Max took off with his cash. It wasn't even the money. It was the fear of missing out on tonight. If it didn't happen tonight, it would never happen. He was certain of it deep in his gut. There had been too many stops and starts in their relationship. It was now or never.

He saw a cab idling at a hydrant a few yards away. He ran to it hopefully. Max was in the front seat, eating a fresh gyro.

"OMG, you waited, thank you." Dane climbed inside and pulled the promised $50 out of his wallet. Max shrugged.

"Keep it. Where to?"

Dane couldn't believe it. This was the first time someone in New York had turned down a tip from him. He eyed Max's gyro. He felt like offering him the $50 for it.

"Thank you, Max! I'm going to 24th and 12th. By the way, that gyro looks delicious. Did you get it at Planet Gyro?"

"Yeah. You want one? We can stop on the way. I wouldn't mind getting a second one for later."

"Actually... yes!" The crappy dinner burger had only scratched his itch for something tasty. "Let's go!"

Max pulled out into traffic and drove to Rector Street, pulling up in front.

"I'm buying, just tell me what you want," Dane said.

"Liver, with a fine chianti and fava beans," Max said.

Dane reared up. "So chicken?"

"That'll be fine, thanks."

He returned a few minutes later with two chicken gyros and sat back happily in the back seat to eat his. The rain had stopped, but the fog was gloomy and cold.

Max drove up Hudson Street. "You going to a club?"

Dane wasn't in the mood. He pretended he didn't hear the cabbie.

"You're going to a club, right?" Max repeated.

"Yeah, yeah, Pummels," Dane said. "It's kind of alternative, kind of... you know, part goth, a little steampunk, kind of..."

"Isn't that one of them **Bee Dee Ess Emmmmm** clubs?" Max said.

Dane froze. "Maybe," he said.

A loud, melodious giggle escaped from Max. "Don't be so uptight. Every cabbie in New York knows Pummels."

That seemed like an odd thing to say. Did Max mean that everyone knew the club because they drove a lot of clients there or because all cabbies went to BDSM clubs?

Dane changed the subject. "Do you know if

we'll be passing a flower shop? I need to get some roses for my friend."

"You're bringing flowers to a BDSM club?" The girlish tee-hee echoed again.

Dane checked Max's taxi license. It said he was born in 1940. Unless Max was a magic elf, there was no way he was in his 70s.

The cab stopped for a red light at a fluorescently bright corner. Max turned around and for the first time Dane saw his driver's face in the light. Max had fresh, glowing skin and long eyelashes. She had a cute dimple in her chin. It took Dane a few seconds to realize she was wearing pale lipstick.

"You're not Max!?"

"I'm Jax."

"What is this," he muttered, "the linguistic Matrix or something?"

"Jax, short for Jacquita. My grandpa Max raised

me so it's always been Max and Jax. I drive for him on weekends."

She pulled off the hat and scarf and a mass of blonde curls fell to her shoulders.

Dane gaped. "Ok, so you're not a man."

"Only if the guy really wants me to be," she shot back.

This made him laugh. "I'm Dane. Very nice to meet you, Jax."

He immediately texted Booker:

"Fun cab ride. Male driver is a she."

Booker answered:

"OK, so what?"

"Not transman. Cis-woman."

"OK, that's different."

"Looks like Butter Queen before she melted."

"Ha! I must meet her. What's her name?"

"Jax Schwartz."

"Jax?! Curly blond hair and dimpled chin?"

"How do you know her??! Omg lol"

Jax turned slowly onto a poorly-lit side-street in Chelsea. The phone signal died, so he slid it back in his pocket. That was freaky. How did Booker know Jax? What did she do when she wasn't driving for her grandfather?

"My friend Booker says he knows you."

"Booker?" She sat up straight. "Booker Dodson?"

"Oh. My. God. You know each other!"

"Don't get your panties in a twist," she said calmly. "Not carnally. Wow, I need to call him."

Dane loved this woman's humor. Lorraine did not have much of a sense of humor. That was one of the things that bothered him. Lorraine never got his jokes, his wordplay, his weird humor. Jax was witty, like Booker. He wondered how their paths had crossed.

The cab bumped along the cobblestones and came to a stop.

"They got the good stuff." Jax pointed a thumb

at the only sign of life, a small florist shop called Rainbow Gardens. "Go on, I'll wait."

Flamingo string lights were wound around tall steel containers of flowers standing under the store's tiny awning. Dane felt oddly comforted that Jax took him to a queer business. When he pushed open the heavy front door, the fragrance of honeysuckle and Sweet Williams swept through his core. He hadn't smelled anything so wonderful since the summer he spent working at the Elkhart plant nursery, potting up stocks and heliotropes.

"Hi, I'm Kevin, may I help you?" a perky man chirped from the counter. Kevin looked out the window. "Did Jax bring you here?"

"You know Jax, too?"

"Everyone who's anyone knows Jax," Kevin said snootily. "OK, darling, so what do we need flowers for on this dark night? Are they for yourself or someone else?

"Someone else."

"And what is this someone else's relationship to you?"

The question threw Dane for a loop. How could he describe it without revealing he was BDSM. Some gay men had a negative attitude towards Leather.

"Well, it's for a cis-woman," he treaded cautiously. "I want to... impress her in a... a romantic way."

"Are they for Jax?!" Kevin got excited. "You can tell me!"

"No!" Dane didn't mean to say it so vehemently.

Kevin cooled to a polite but chilly tone. "Do you know what you want?"

"I guess a dozen roses." Dane felt foolish. Roses were so cliché. "Unless you recommend something else?"

"I always recommend these when I have them in." Kevin showed him a container of white lilies.

"Aren't those for funerals?"

"Don't blame flowers for how people use them!"

"I guess I never thought of it that way." He felt that Kevin was disappointed in him. "I know roses are predictable."

"Predictability isn't bad if it works," Kevin said, putting on gloves to wrap a dozen long-stem red roses for him and ringing up the bill. "That'll be $60.66."

Dane walked back to the cab, feeling stupid. Here he wanted to impress Lorraine with his creativity, and all he could think to get were a common valentine bouquet. He sucked.

"Great shop, thanks," he mumbled getting back into the cab.

"You look overjoyed," Jax pursed her lips.

"No, I mean, it was nice in there. Kevin was nice too." Dane checked his phone. There was a text from Booker asking where he went.

"Lost signal. Text from club soon."

Jax took a sharp turn and Dane fell on top of the rose bouquet.

"OWWW!" A thorn stuck him on the lower lip, breaking the skin. He licked off the blood, feeling sorry for himself. He'd look like he had a herpes cold sore. Meanwhile, his ass still felt unaccountably damp. The seam in his pants were pulling on him so tight it hurt to sit up straight.

"Now what?" Jax said. "I hear you whimpering back there."

"One of the rose thorns stuck my lip bad."

"So you're on the thorns of a dilemma?"

She cracked herself up, snorting and squealing in delight. She was so adorable he almost started laughing with her. Almost.

Dane suddenly realized why he had designated the pants he was wearing for emergency use only. They had a particularly irritating seam that rubbed him raw from taint to spine. He decided they were ideal for work, where he always wore thick BVDs, which provided enough insulation to let him get through the day fairly comfortably. But the fetish undies were paper-thin and a burning welt was spreading across his ass. He pulled on the crotch, trying to readjust the seam.

"How do you know Booker?" He chatted while his fingers covertly plucked.

"Ah, funny story. We went to Montessori together as kids, lost track, and then we found each other again at Pride, and then we worked for Obama together. Haven't talked to him since the Trump election debacle. How do you know him?"

"I live with him," he said.

"Ohh. Oho. So are you bi?" she asked. "I mean, you're buying flowers for your girlfriend."

"Not my girlfriend," he corrected her.

"Ah. So they are for your dominatrix?"

"Why would you even say that!" he protested in embarrassment.

"Because you're going to Pummels with roses and I do not think you are a top." She smiled at him in the rearview mirror. "I guessed right, didn't I?"

"How about you?" He precipitously changed the subject. "Are you bi? Lesbian? Pansexual?"

"Mmmm..." She seemed to be considering it. "I'm trisexual. If boobs, behinds or penises are involved, I'm sexual."

She made him grin. "If only everyone in the BDSM Scene was as open-minded as you."

"Yeah, the Scene," she said, sighing. "That's another story. Did you hear about that dominatrix on Long Island? Fucking shame."

"It looks so bad for the Community," he said.

"Fuck that." Her voice grew an edge. "The Community will survive but what about the victims? Will they ever trust a Femdom again? I bet she has other victims who'll never even tell anyone what she did to them. Men are so ashamed of being victims." She exhaled loudly. "People like her poison the well for the good guys."

"You are so right!" He felt angry but freed at the same time. You couldn't blame BDSMers for being the victims of predators and phonies. BDSMers were some of the finest humans he'd ever known. He needed to remember that during dark times. It was like blaming flowers, wasn't it?

He flashed to Goddess Memory, the first dom he served. She still walked around events with her little clique, acting like the queen of everything. He was so ashamed of what a doormat he was with her that he never told anyone, not even Booker, how he let her treat him. That was a different Dane, a man who settled for the crumbs any dom tossed at him just for an opportunity to get some play. He knew better now.

"I have a bad memory myself," he said ironically, knowing Jax wouldn't get it, but amusing himself.

He texted Booker:

> "I think the cab ride is changing my life."

> "Are you crushing on Jax?"

> "What? No. But she's cool af."

As the cab rolled up to the club, Dane scanned the street intensely. No sign of Lorraine. He did it! She usually arrived at 9 pm and it was 8:48. He beat her by 12 minutes. Now he could relax.

"Thank you for everything, Jax. I wish I could ride with you all the way up town. You're amazing. I hope I see you again."

"Thanks," she said. "Good luck with whoever she is. We all deserve to find our joy."

"We do," he breathed.

"We do," she repeated. "Now get the hell out."

๛ Chapter 4 ๙

COOKIE MONSTER

Dane leaned against the club wall out front and waited patiently, playing a game on his mobile. Maybe he would kneel for her right there on the sidewalk outside the club marquee. That would definitely take it to a new level, doing it in public. At 9:20, he got restless and walked up and down the street.

The bouquet was starting to fall apart. It was crushed from his fall in the cab. Buds had broken off and a few blooms were flattened. He trimmed it and tried to disguise a tear in the tissue paper. It was 9:30 now and still no sign of Lorraine.

He spotted a couple he knew as Master Terry and Slave Pirate walking out of the club holding hands.

"Hi," he said as he dashed to them, "have you seen Lorraine?"

"Oh God, yeah," Pirate said, rolling her eyes.

"Inside?" The roses shook in agitation and a few petals dropped.

Pirate was about to ask Dane a question, but Terry put his hand on her arm and shook his head.

"What do you mean, Dane?" he asked.

"Did she go inside?"

"Uh... we... don't know?" Pirate said, looking up at Terry.

"We don't know anything about it," Terry said firmly.

Dane's cell dinged. It was Booker. He waved at them and walked away to text with him.

"U at club yet?"

"Just now. No sign of Lorraine. Weird. What are you up to?"

"Jer just got here. We're peeling ginger."

Dane felt a twinge of envy. He wouldn't mind being home, partying with Booker and his cooking school wife, Jerome. Jer came by on weekends to prep, chop and prepare feasts with Booker every weekend. Jer was a professional kickboxer, built like a kangaroo, with a lean torso and powerful legs. He'd strip off his clothes the minute he walked in and change into pantyhose and heels.

At first, Book acted shocked, but Dane could tell he was charmed by it.

"Aw, yeah, that's how to do it, mate!" Jer whistled at Book a few weeks later when he donned girdle and brassiere to cook alongside his friend.

Dane was there that night. He'd never seen Booker in fetish mode until then. He couldn't stop watching the two chefs. They were bizarrely enchanting. They shared some madcap culinary spiritual energy that made it seem as if they were performing a choreographed kitchen dance. When the show was over, they sat together around the table, drinking Barolo and Monastrell, toasting each other's health, and eating as noisily as they laughed.

The next day, Dane and Booker both agreed that Jer was an amazing new addition to their extended family of friends.

"I could come home."

"You could. But it would be better if you came late."

"Jerry doesn't know yet - he's on my menu for 2nite."

"Really! I didn't know it was going there."

Dane walked away from the club for privacy. Book and Jerry getting it on!! While this was sudden, it made sense. They'd discussed polyamory and polyfidelity. It was inevitable they'd have to evolve so Dane could have a Mistress and Book could have his husband and all of them could live in poly harmony. He didn't know how to feel about it now that the moment had arrived.

"Your decision about Lorraine made me decide to risk it."

He stared at his friend's text, and remembered how Book had given him his blessing to pursue

Lorraine just this morning, and Booker didn't even like Lorraine.

"I hope it's great for you, Book. Don't do anything I wouldn't do."

"I plan to do all the things you wouldn't do!"

"LOL later. Low battery."

Dane's cell was down to 15%. He turned it off. Funny how things work. A year ago, Jer moving into their lives would have scared him. Now he just saw it as them moving forward as a family and becoming a bigger family. That was a good thing.

When he got back to the club entrance, Terry and Pirate were gone, but a guy in a red latex cape and full rubber hood was leaning against the wall, smoking a cigarette through the mouth hole.

"Do you know Mistress Lorraine?" Dane asked him.

"Are you a cop? A reporter?" The hole blew smoke at him. "I'm a lawyer. I know my rights."

"Never mind," Dane sighed and walked away, pacing indecisively on the sidewalk. It was closing in on 10pm. Maybe Lorraine got in early. Maybe she was already ass-deep in male subs while he'd waited like an idiot on the street. The fantasy he had constructed all day, about throwing himself at her feet on the sidewalk and scattering rose petals before her to show her she was his queen, was gone. And his ass hurt like hell.

It was time to go inside. He pushed the heavy door, and was blinded by the darkness for a moment. But soon his eyes adjusted to the dim lighting. He could almost taste the smell of leather mixed with sweat and sawdust that lay just ahead, beyond a pair of leather-upholstered doors.

In one spot, a wall panel was set in deeper than the others. He paused to remember how Memory had wrestled him into the narrow recess once, covering him with her body, clenching his hair in her fist, growling that he belonged to her, and pressing her knee into his groin until he swooned. His pants got tight. He wanted to feel that again, but with a better person than she turned out to be.

The burning welt by his crack stung like a hornet. His knees almost buckled. He forced himself to straighten up and walked ahead, suffering with every step. He pushed the heavy swinging door wide open, hoping no one could see the tears in his eyes. If only the welt between his legs was something a dominant had done to him, a sharp stroke of a cruel whip that landed right down the crack of his ass, he was sure it wouldn't hurt as much. Or not in the same way. He tried hard to put himself in that fantasy, where the pain from the seam was the handiwork of a sexy sadist and not a sloppy seamstress.

"So good to see you, Dane!" A petite brunette flung her arms around him and hugged him tight. "I'm so glad you came tonight," she said.

"Thanks, Irina!" Dane stooped and kissed the top of her head. "How are you?"

"I'm good." Irina parted the crowd to let him see the show. She softly squeezed his hand. "Are you okay?"

"I'm great!" He tried to sound upbeat but his ass was slowly murdering him. He just wanted to find Lorraine.

"Nice jacket!" she felt the leather on Booker's jacket. "So soft. Ahh, your boyfriend treats you good, doesn't he?"

"It's just a loaner," Booker smiled. But it was true. His boyfriend treated him royally.

"Why do you have roses?" She looked puzzled.

He pretended he didn't hear her, instead pointing at a large woman sprawled like a child over a little man's lap. He had pulled her pink ruffled panties down to her ankles and was making her count each spank he delivered to her ample, creamy rump.

"Why is Shastie with John?" he asked.

"It's John's 50th birthday," Irina whispered. "He's giving anyone who wants 50 spanks and one for good luck, their choice of hand or paddle." Irina smiled from ear to ear. "It's so cute."

Dane grinned. "Shastie looks happy."

"This is like her third turn! I don't know how John's arm can keep up with spanking sluts like her." She said it loudly, so Shastie could hear her.

"You're just jealous," Shastie called out while the crowd laughed.

"Maybe I should get in line next?" Irina teased.

John spoke up, "A brat like you should go straight to the front of the line." The kinksters who were patiently waiting their turn started pushing Irina to the front, hooting and clapping, while she pretended to resist them.

Dane left them to their fun and searched the crowd. He'd never seen the club so packed. Lorraine could be at her favorite spot, all the way at the back and around a few corners. It might take him another half an hour to find her in this crowd.

He drifted into a mass of men standing near a cross, wondering if Lorraine could be behind the wall of burly shoulders. Instead, a male dominant was working over a woman with clawed gloves and clothespins. The woman arched backwards, her eyes filled with narcotic euphoria, as her top clamped her nipples and her lower lip. When he ran his claws down her naked thighs, she stretched so high that she appeared to be climbing to heaven.

A man dressed in heavy chains hopped up to him, hobbled by the weight and confinement.

"Brother, where have you been?" It was Geoff. Just as Jer was Book's cooking wife, Geoff was Dane's BDSM equivalent. They attended all the national events together, organized some fundraisers together, and occasionally did demos together with Geoff's master, a big beautiful bear named Brian.

Dane gave him a ferocious hug. "WOOF!"

"Woof yourself, it's not fair when I can't hug back!"

"Yeah, I feel so sorry for you." Dane smirked.

Geoff's relationship with his Master was so beautiful, everyone wanted to be close to them, but they were very picky. Dane felt really special that they cared so much about him. They were two of the sweetest men he knew, apart from Book. Master Brian was the living definition of a Leather God: a towering man covered in thick luxurious curls, with a stoic slightly aloof demeanor. When he liked you, his toothy smile was as big as his great big heart. Dane crushed on him a little, but he and Geoff were into a level of play that intimidated Dane in its raw intensity.

"Are you okay?" Geoff asked slowly. "Like really ok?"

"Yeah, sure, why?"

"What happened to your lip?"

Dane self-consciously touched the aching bump from the rose's sting. "Got kissed by a vampire."

Geoff didn't laugh, which made him uneasy.

"What's with the flowers?" Geoff asked.

"Don't tell anyone, ok? They're for Lorraine," Dane said. "Have you seen her?"

"What do you mean?"

Dane leaned in conspiratorially and said, "Tonight's the night, Geoff. I'm going to beg to be her permanent slave."

"OMG, Dane. OMG." He looked horrified. "No."

"I know you're not her fan, but it's the right thing for me. I'm ready for what you and Brian have."

"Uhhhh... are you serious? Now?"

"I'm dead serious. Why are you acting so surprised?" True, he'd bitched to Geoff about her, and they'd talked about all his doubts, but Geoff knew he'd been feeling more optimistic lately, more willing to commit.

"I gotta go, Master's waiting. The crew's hanging in the dome of silence. Come talk to us, ok?" Geoff hopped off in the direction of Brian before Dane had time to say anything more. That seemed odd.

There was no sign of Lorraine anywhere. The cages lined up on one wall were all empty, which was strange, especially on such a busy night. Come to think of it, other than John's birthday spanking party and the top clamping his sub, no one seemed to be utilizing any of the large-scale equipment. The suspension bondage rig was deserted, the bondage wheel was still, and the birdcage was parked on the floor with someone sitting cross-legged inside it, texting on their phone.

"Nobody's playing tonight," said a short guy wearing sparkly red Mary Janes and a tight red PVC jumpsuit that showed off his poochy belly. It was Billy, an accountant by day and a disco queen with a penchant for whippings by Friday and Saturday nights, when he was always among the first to arrive and the last to leave at Pummels.

"What's up, Billy?" Dane gave him a light shoulder punch.

"That fucking Marmalade disaster. Everyone's afraid we'll be raided tonight."

"Why would they come here? They already busted her, right?"

"Any excuse to bust a BDSM space," Billy said. "They just look for excuses to torture us."

Linette, a lesbian dom friend, walked into the middle of their conversation. Dane liked her a lot. She had a wild gray mane of hair that swept to her shoulders and eyes so dark they looked like thunderclouds. She was a retired cop, very earnest, but also very motherly towards subs.

"No, it's because they need to build the case for the DA," she corrected Billy, "They'd be right to interview as many male subs as possible to see if there are other victims. They need to collect evidence the DA can use."

"Really?" Dane looked around curiously. "Think some of her patsies are among us?"

Billy snorted. "Ya think, Dane? Ya think maybe at least ONE person in this VAST crowd could possibly have been rooked by her?"

"Wow!" said Dane.

"Wow," said Billy.

"Be nice," Linette slapped Billy's hand.

"Yes, Ma'am," Billy bowed his head.

Dane instinctively looked around the room, as if he could spot a victim by the way he looked. He noticed one guy restlessly pacing back and forth near the dressing area, hands crammed in his pockets, avoiding eye contact with anyone who passed. He looked drugged, agitated, a little crazed. Then Dane realized he was jerking off inside his pants. Euw.

"Catch you later." Dane excused himself.

He wandered further into the depths of the club, back to the darkest rooms at the end of a cramped hall with exposed ceiling pipes. In the way back, people forgot everything outside the alternate realities they were creating for themselves.

He knew he wouldn't find Lorraine there. She said it was too claustrophobic for her back there. Dane suspected she just couldn't handle the energy of the hard-core players in back. Their interactions were primal, sometimes extreme. Not everyone could handle BDSM at that level. He wanted to drench himself in it. To him, these people were revolutionaries, the real champions of pleasure, pushing themselves further than other people would even conceive of going. He knew he could be one of them if he had the chance.

Whizzzz. Cattails flew through the air. *THWACK*, lashes fell on flesh. A shrill scream pierced the shadows.

He squeezed his way through the crowd, passing spectral figures giving themselves fully to strange pleasures. Moans and whimpers emanated from otherwise silent nooks, some of them bare except for hooks on the walls and players acting out their fantasies, some in leather, others in fetish gear, a few stark naked. Back here, where the atmosphere was fraught with sexual tension, where leather and steel glinted and faces glistened with sweat, it was all about going deep into yourself, as deep as a human can safely go, to the limits of endurance. Primal passions were embraced without false modesty or toxic shame.

In one nook, there was a fully mummified figure lying bound and immobile on a steel table, a female dressed head to toe in black latex focused on him, and constantly checking his safety. In another, a solitary naked woman in a tall stiff collar was slowly riding a Sybian she had mounted on a bench, as hungry to be seen by voyeurs as they were eager to crowd outside her nook for a glimpse of her solo ride.

He walked back out to the main area and headed toward the blinding lights of the bar. Lorraine wasn't anywhere. It was useless to search. Still he was afraid to ditch the roses until he had proof. He ordered a cup of orange juice from the bar and sat down to nurse it, trying to decide if he should just call it a night and go home to Booker or stick around and hang with his crew. He should probably at least go to say hi to them.

He turned on his phone and waved it around, looking for a signal. The battery was down to 12%. If he had an emergency later, he might be screwed. He shut it off again and turned to watch the shoe and boot stations across from him.

The shoeshine benches were doing brisk business, with doms of all genders politely standing in line. None of this crowd was worried about getting arrested. Dane thought that was so funny because, as a fellow footie, he got harder watching a hot boy deliver an immaculate shine and finish with a boot licking than watching a spanking.

He liked spankings because they subsumed pain, humiliation and powerlessness, the trifecta of his sexual submission. But watching someone lick the boots of their Master or, oh my good god, being the boot-licker, that was like getting on a rocket ship to a new reality, a journey fueled by an electric explosion that lit every circuit in his brain and made his genitals twitch from taint to tip.

"Dane." Someone was calling to him. "Dane, honey!"

Lucy walked up to him at the bar and hugged him. Lucy always wore nipple-defying corsets. Tonight's crimson velvet model kept deliciously threatening to reveal an areola every time she sighed deeply. She was the oldest and most experienced kinkster in his crew.

Lucy was married to another kinky person for 27 years. Master Mark, a pale, soft-spoken, much older man, died of chronic kidney disease two years ago. When Dane met him, he was already weak and confined to a wheelchair. He couldn't get his chair past the swinging door, so Brian would carry him in while Lucy and George folded the heavy chair and carried it in. Watching big bear Brian gently place Mark back in his chair always made Dane's heart full. All that caring and commitment. It was so BDSM.

Shiree, a wide-hipped brunette who wore Harry Potter glasses, joined them. She was somewhere on the Asperger's spectrum, which made her habitually earnest and socially awkward. She had been searching for years for her "Prince Charming Bondage," as she called him, someone who would tie her to the bed every night.

Dane introduced her to her ex-dom, Robert and at first, they seemed like a happy couple. After that didn't work out, Robert confided that, while he really liked her, she was a dud in the dungeon.

"No matter how you tie her, she has only one question," he said, "'How else will you tie me?' Christ. 'How else will you tie me?' I like bondage as much as the next dom, but that's her whole scene, tie her up and sit there until she falls asleep. Then when she wakes up, untie her and tie her in a different position. Over and over again. The phrase has scarred my brain. 'How else will you tie me? How else will you tie me?' That's a lot of work for nothing."

"Nothing? Not even a blowjob?"

"Not even a "Thank you, Master." It was, like, am I there dominating this woman or am I just a robot who exists to tie her up?"

Dane didn't judge her. He was amused by Robert's story and decided not to introduce her to any other friends, but he didn't hold it against her. Everybody had their reasons for liking what they liked, and everybody deserved to find that person who liked it too so they could be happy together.

When Lorraine started coming to the club, Dane's friendship with Shiree got weird, because she immediately disliked Lorraine. He could sense it though she didn't say anything about it. He wondered if Lorraine was too extroverted for his introverted friend, or if Shiree was jealous he'd found his Dominant while she was still looking.

Shiree finally admitted that she didn't want to watch his scenes anymore because there was too much diva and not enough sadomasochist in Lorraine. Shiree said she could tell that Lorraine looked down on submissives, like they were really beneath her. That really hurt Dane. What was worse is that he knew Shiree wasn't completely wrong.

Lorraine was the self-styled Kim Kardashian of SM. She was always the most fashionably dressed woman at the club. She wore outrageous fetish dresses and boots. Her hair was platinum blonde one week, copper red the next. Sometimes she matched her hair to her outfit, and dyed it blue or purple. She sported a bored, distant facial expression most of the time, as if she'd seen it all and done it all. Her make-up was so heavily layered she looked almost like a Drag Queen, all contoured planes and creamy skin.

One thing make-up couldn't disguise was her magnificent nose. It was large and hawk-like. When she stared down at you, her nostrils looked like caves of infinity about to suck you in. He was captivated by her self-confidence, her shameless exhibitionism, her haughty attitudes.

Several years back, he promised Lorraine he'd play with her exclusively in exchange for her putting him under consideration to be her permanent slave. The probationary period started out as three months, then went to six months, and now it was almost three years. He had wanted to break the impasse, but now it seemed to be a hopeless quest. He remembered his dragon fantasy. The morning was a lifetime ago. In retrospect, it seemed childish and idiotic, nothing but a stoned, transitory illusion.

"Come on, Dane," Lucy said warmly, touching his shoulder. "Let's go see Brian."

Dejected, he let Lucy and Shiree link arms with him and lead him to a round table near some exposed ductwork which constantly hummed. The club's noise was muffled and conversation was muted here, making it a perfect dead zone for private conversation.

Brian and Geoff were talking with Irina and George, an old play-partner of Lucy and Mark's who had moved into their home when Mark was dying. George ended up staying after Mark's passing so he could help Lucy care for her disabled son, who had inherited Mark's health problems. George was a good soul. He bathed and fed Lucy's son like he was his own child and took him to movies. The whole crew went out of its way to include Lucy's kid in G-rated outings when possible, taking him to parks and concerts. That's how kind his crew was. He was proud to be one of them.

"Woof," Dane said, cheered to see them. "Hello, darlings!"

Brian gazed at him affectionately. Dane had seen those eyes paralyze subs during Scenes with their icy intensity. Tonight, they were mild and gentle.

Irina started. "We need to talk to you about Lorraine," she said.

"Oh?" This put Dane on guard. Were they staging some kind of intervention to stop him from asking to serve Lorraine? She never did fit in with his friends, but he didn't realize they actually worried about him being with her. Well, ok, maybe they did, maybe they were a little overly pleased that time he broke up with her, but an intervention? Seriously?

"We're glad to see you, Dane." Brian looked at him as if trying to read his mind. "We weren't sure if you'd be here tonight." The women pushed Dane down into a chair next to Brian and arranged themselves around the small table. As soon as everyone was seated, Brian began, "We assumed you already knew, but Geoff said you don't so we felt we should tell you as soon as possible."

"What?" Dane said.

"Lorraine is Marmalade," Brian said.

"What?" Dane had no idea what Brian meant by that. "What?" It was like something failed to load in his brain and he was stuck on the word.

"What? What?" he repeated.

Brian said it in a louder voice. "Lorraine is Marmalade."

Everyone was looking at him. Dane couldn't move his jaw.

"Marmalade Loretta," he finally choked out. His tongue felt like it didn't belong to him. "Noooo."

"I so thought you knew!" Geoff blurted. He looked like he was going to cry, and Brian put an arm around him to hold him together.

Irina couldn't hold back now. She reported with vicious glee, "She had 8 different identities online, 2 on FetLife, and the rest on KEEN and Seeking Arrangements," she snorted. "She did

FinDom sessions as Marmalade. They say she stole from clients she conned into investing in some kind of cookie scam."

Lucy reached into her bag for a candy bar and started eating it. "Cookie scam!" She shook her head. "Psycho bitch qu'est-ce que c'est."

"What's a FinDom?" Shiree asked. "Is that a scuba diving fetish?"

"Oh my God." Lucy covered her mouth with both hands to stop chocolate chunks from spewing.

"It's a seal scene. She puts on rubber fins and barks," George cracked.

"Don't listen to him!" Lucy rolled her eyes at George, then explained it to Shiree. "It's where a prodom makes a sub give her expensive gifts and extra cash. The Fin is for Financial. It's like prodom plus, where you get paid a lot more to do a lot less, but you threaten them you'll tell their wives or bosses, and they give you more money."

"Why wasn't I born dom?" Shiree asked the table. "I could so do that job."

"Let's get back to Dane's problem." Brian said. Everyone got quiet and looked at Dane. "What's done is done," Brian said. "None of us think any less of you, Dane. But now you need to move on and cut her out of your heart. We'll do whatever you need us to do to help you get through this."

Brian leaned across the table and covered Dane's hand with his hairy paw. They made a pile of hands to show Dane their unified love and support.

"We're here for you, brother," Geoff murmured, and the others nodded and agreed.

Dane was numb. He could not make sense of it. How could the gorgeous platinum blonde who swore to him she had no other slaves be the Long Island cookie-baker who scammed her submissives?

"You're lucky she didn't suck you dry, bro," Geoff tried to console Dane, "She didn't just steal 180 thousand for her business, she stole MILLIONS, making clients buy her designer purses and fancy fetish outfits and pay for expensive vacations."

"Soooo disgusting," Irina said. "I hope they put her away for a long time."

"I don't understand this," Dane said. "I don't understand any of this."

Brian sighed. "Reality hasn't sunken in yet. Dane, a lot of us get burned at some point but... this... the way you are finding out... this is all very unfortunate. We were so sure you knew until Geoff told us about the flowers. That's why I could not let you keep walking around the club looking for Lorraine."

"The person we knew as Lorraine who wasn't Lorraine," Shiree pointed out.

Dane was too shaken to speak. The superior woman of his dreams was lowlife Marmalade, the stuff of nightmares. Of course she was. He knew Marmalade looked familiar. He'd just never seen her without her mask of thick makeup. Why didn't he recognize her big nose? Maybe it didn't look as majestic on Loretta as it did on Lorraine.

"What about the hair? Loretta is a brunette." He felt ashamed as soon as the words left his mouth. Why was he still holding on?

"Dane, come on," Geoff cringed. "You had to know those were wigs. She was so fake even her hair was fake."

Brian found the silver lining. "It's not the worst burn. Not by any means the worst. She didn't physically hurt you, right?" He paused, trying to read Dane's mood. "What can I say? We're grieving for you, Dane."

"We are," his friends echoed. "How could she do this to you? Fuck her," they repeated again and again.

"Fuck that phony baloney," Shiree said. "You can do better."

A burning coal ignited in his head. The flame started at his right temple and fanned out across his scalp, ear to ear. It was as if someone was tightening a metal cap around his skull. His eyes felt like they'd explode from the pressure. This was the worst migraine he'd had since the night his parents died.

Brian saw Dane's distress and spoke calmly, with conviction. "You're going to be okay, Dane. You'll get through this. Give it some time."

"I'll call you tomorrow." Dane jumped to his feet. "I need to talk to Booker, I need to tell him."

The rush from standing suddenly made him feel as if an axe was splitting his head in two. He gripped his head with both hands.

Geoff stood up and rushed to him, grabbing his arm. "Are you having a migraine again? Can I get you something? Don't go, Dane, we're here for you. You don't have to leave."

"I'm fine," he lied, "I'm fine."

"Stay with us," they all entreated him. "We'll go for coffee and ice cream."

"No!" Dane stubbornly insisted. "I'm sorry. I have to go."

Brian sat back in his chair. "Let him go, Geoff. Dane needs room to process this," he said quietly. "Let's give him that space."

Geoff looked into Dane's eyes.

"You sure you'll be okay, brother?" he asked.

"Yes, I'm going home," Dane said. "Thank you," he said to the table, "Thank all of you. I love you guys. I need to see Booker. I'll text you tomorrow. Promise."

By the time he got to the street, he didn't know what to do with himself.

How could he have been so stupid? How could he have ignored all the signs? How did he add two plus two and come up with three thousand? What the fuck was wrong with him? He was still holding the fucking bouquet. He threw the flowers to the ground and stomped them into confetti.

In the dark quiet of the rain-washed street, the stinging pain in his temple began to subside. But not the pain in his soul. That would never subside. He would never get over this, never.

He was done with dominatrices, totally done. He would never trust another dominant woman again. They really were all like his mother, mean, evil bitches only looking out for themselves. He was fucking done. Thank God his friends saved him from making an even bigger fool of himself.

ᴃᴐ Chapter 5 ᴄ୫

DESSERTS

His scalp was burning as hot as the welt between his legs. Each step hurt from skull to groin now. He pulled out his phone and cursed it at the top of his lungs for not loading fast enough. There were dozens of texts from Booker. He was afraid of draining the battery completely so just texted quickly.

"I'm dying. Migraine. Lorraine. OMG."

"OMG! I knew she was a mess. OMG."

"OMG I'm such an idiot."

"Don't do that to yourself. It's not your fault."

"I'm dead inside."

"I'll come get you."

"No!"

"You sure?"

"I need to breathe. I'll walk home."

"It's ugly out there tonight."

"I'm from Iowa, I can handle a little snow."

"You sure?"

"I'm down to 6% on my phone. I love you."

His phone beeped a power warning and he turned it off. He didn't know where to go. He wasn't ready to go home. Booker would try to climb into his head and Jerome would go to a corner and do squats in his pantyhose.

Dane didn't want to talk to anyone about anything. He'd wept enough tears for a lifetime. He was through with crying. Fuck her. She was a lying whore and he was just another one of her patsies. Nothing good could have ever come of it, no matter what happened. If she had turned him down, he would have kept pining for her, hanging on to the belief that she alone possessed that special something that could fill the wound in his soul. He would have nurtured an infantile fantasy that she would rectify him, redeem him and reward him for all his suffering, and given him a true love that surpassed all other loves. What a friggin moron he was.

He remembered all the times she said things that bothered him. Like that time she came down hard on him for still playing with Geoff and Brian when he was also bottoming to her. She said he was gay and he heard himself say, "Club bisexuality isn't the same as bisexuality in other places." It mollified her somewhat, but he felt like a skunk for not using that moment to come out and tell her he'd sucked hundreds of dicks and still wasn't gay.

He was a fucking idiot. Not just for falling for her shallow opinions and generalized bullshit, but for investing so completely in his own bullshit about her, the bullshit that made him thirst for her like she was a fine wine instead of warm beer in a rusty can.

There was no perfect Mistress. He imagined her serving cookies like a 1950s housewife, probably with the same preening attitude and 18 layers of make-up to hide her wrinkle-puss. Loretta Lanzetti probably had a pimply ass and tits flat as pancakes and pussy lips that hung to her knees.

And if he fell for a big fat phony, didn't that make him one too? The man who thought he was much too smart to fall for a con artist had walked around the club all night with a bouquet in his hands, like a pathetic schmuck, while everyone laughed behind his back. Now it all made sense: why Terry and Pirate got confused about him asking if Lorraine was "inside." They thought he meant "inside" like the slang for being in prison. And that's why Billy made the crack about there being at least one more of her victims at the club. Now he understand that Linette hushed Billy to protect Dane's feelings. She'd pitied him. Tears rolled down his cheeks.

Why didn't they just tell him? He was suddenly pissed at everyone who was too chickenshit to tell him and equally angry at Brian for telling him. Brian could have broken the news more gently. King Kong would have broken the news better! Why didn't Geoff tell him the minute they bumped into each other instead of running back to tell on him to Brian and leaving it up to his Master to do the dirty work? Geoff should've told him straight up! Then it wouldn't have turned into that humiliating kinky kaffee klatch, where everyone could secretly gloat that they warned him about Lorraine.

He started walking east, then changed his mind and walked west, crossing the street so he wouldn't pass under the club's marquee. The street was surreal and he wasn't even high. It looked like a cardboard movie set he could destroy with his fists. The cramped building facades sagged into each other like tired old men.

He remembered the shoes! If the cops showed up and searched his bag, they'd find the special "Chicshoebox" Lincoln used for the photo shoots. She probably had dozens of their in-house company boxes in her closets. That would be the end for him. Everything would be revealed. His perversions. His fetishes. His gay sugar daddy! Booker's father would not be too pleased if he found out that his son often blew as much money on Dane in a month as Dane paid him in rent.

He noticed a dumpster near a doorway down the street, and strode quickly towards it, looking over his shoulder to check for people watching. A cab drove by slowly, lights off, and he ducked behind the dumpster, waiting until it turned uptown at the corner. He frenziedly pulled things out of his backpack, at last finding the box of shoes at the very bottom.

He ditched the box into the dumpster and sprinted away, trying to ignore the pain that was ripping him apart. Fuck Lorraine. Fuck her and fuck her shoes. She almost fucking ruined his life. He hated her.

When he first got to New York, he met a sub guy named Andy. The nicest guy in the world, one of the good guys. One day, Andy went to see his regular Mistress of many years for a "bondage special" she was running. Two other clients were in separate rooms, and all three of them were nicely trussed up and relaxed when the doorbell rang. Suddenly, there was a big commotion. Andy heard an angry man, shouting and threatening violence when the Mistress told him he couldn't enter without an appointment and that bondage was not a walk-in service.

Andy told Dane what it was like to be manacled to a wall while a stranger in the next room, apparently armed, threatened to murder your dominatrix.

"She kept saying, 'Just put down the gun, Frankie, just put down the gun.'" Andy recounted. "I thought I was gonna shit blood or stroke out, I was so scared."

Then Andy heard her scream out, "Not the dildos, Frankie!"

The intruder was pitching BDSM toys out the window and onto the busy Manhattan street below. Ironically, the sex toys saved the day. When butt plugs started raining on the sidewalk, passersby panicked and called 911. The cops arrived to find one guy sitting on the sidewalk, still dazed by a huge double-headed dildo that had landed on his head.

When they got upstairs, the cops were able to talk the intruder down and put him in cuffs before anyone got hurt. They took the sobbing dominatrix to a hospital for sedation, freed the bound clients, and let them go home after brief interviews.

At first, Andy thought nobody would ever find out about it. Just another weird thing that happens in the city that never sleeps. Then the evening Post headlines blared "Terrorized Dominatrix Screams for Help as Cops Bust Dungeon of Death." That was all it took for Andy's life to be over. The reporters got his name from the cops and boom. Andy got fired, lost his house, and lost his custody battle with his ex. Andy was so traumatized by the experience, he left New York. Dane lost track of him after that.

His head swelled with pain. So Lorraine was the Cookie Lady even though Loretta Lanzetti looked twice as old and half as attractive as Mistress Lorraine. She took him good. Maybe not like her other victims, but he had lent her a couple of hundred here and there that she never paid back. He bought her toys she never used on him and a latex skirt he never saw her wear. Then there were all the shoes he'd given her! He never considered the money and gifts a cost of services. He thought he was being a good sub and pampering her out of devotion. He got a thrill out of it, just like all those other guys. The feeling that a beautiful woman can take whatever she wants from you and you have no choice but to submit, that was so hot.

But maybe it was also stupid and intrinsically wrong. He didn't consent to it. Did he? He never consented to being with a criminal, that was for sure. On the other hand, maybe he was guilty for playing along and closing his eyes to her shenanigans.

He turned up his collar and headed north on 12th Avenue. The fog was now a biting frost. It brought a flurry of light snow that formed a fine crust on the sidewalk. It reminded him of Iowa. When he was a boy, he would take long walks through the fields behind his parents' home on frosty nights like this. He would wait until he heard snores from their bedroom, and then creep out of the house in stockinged feet, pulling on his heavy corduroy jacket and thin work boots when he got to the front porch.

He'd rove for hours. His first stop was the dilapidated barn where the animals that came with the place still lived. There was a surly old horse named Ben and a Polish chicken named Fifi la Fluff. The horse was a tough character who would bite you and laugh about it but Fifi was a sweet little hen. She hopped on his arm when he visited the barn, gently pecking his shirt pocket to find the dinner scraps he saved for her.

He felt reborn on those chilly, crystalline nights. The stench of summer was gone, along with the flies and bugs that thrived on death and decay. The sweet clean smell of unspoiled earth filled his nostrils. He pretended that the family farm extended for miles and miles, hundreds of miles, like it was his dominion, and he was its Prince.

He loved marching through the icy fields when every step made a crunch. He was a giant, a general, a conqueror. Sometimes, he was a soldier off to war, marching stiffly through frozen rows, a beat-up helmet he found in the attic on his head. Sometimes, he was Frankenstein's monster, arms out, knees stiff. Sometimes he was just Dane, stopping to stare at the cosmos and seeing how many stars he could identify.

Dane wished he was there now, standing in empty fields under wide open skies. He felt more connected to the universe then, part of a larger plan. Even this morning he knew what he would do for the rest of his life. This evening, he knew nothing and felt nothing. Maybe Booker and Jer would hit it off so well, they wouldn't want him around anymore. Anything was possible. He thought back to the poor guy on the train, the one who had so frighteningly fallen from grace that he coveted the donut in a stranger's hands.

He reconsidered his decision to walk back to the Ansonia. It was almost five miles. The more he walked, the more it hurt to walk. He didn't know what to do. He didn't want to waste his battery whining to Booker or risk ruining his friend's romantic evening.

He looked up and made out the North Star and the Little Bear. At least the cosmos hadn't changed. No, really, nothing had changed, had it? He was the same loser having another miserable disappointment with yet another woman. What else was new?

Maybe he was more like his brother, Tim, than he wanted to admit. As much as Lorraine broke his heart, there was another part of him that felt freed, even relieved. He was a callous son-of-a-bitch, a real Jenson, true to his icy Nordic blood.

He walked another half a mile without seeing a single cab pass. He didn't know how much further he could go without crumpling to the ground. He reminded himself that things could be worse. Imagine if he already had vowed to be her slave. He wouldn't be able to duck and run then. He'd be in the thick of it, involved in raising her bail and helping with her legal costs and God knew what else. Brian was right. He had to cut her out of his heart.

He could not walk another step. He dropped his backpack and sat on the icy sidewalk. The frost immediately soothed the screaming welt under his pants and numbed the pain. It felt so good, he almost passed out from the relief. He laid flat on his back, wiggling his hips like a dog in snow, trying to get deliverance from the pain that had spread from his spine to his balls.

In his Iowa boyhood, in the frozen fields out back, he once tested himself to see how long he could stand the cold before he'd have to give up and race back to the house. Now he was a man, and made of sterner stuff. He inhaled the icy air like a Zen master, putting his body in a state of stillness.

He used meditation techniques Book had taught him. He imagined himself cleaning a sacred room, diligently sweeping cobwebs and dead flies out of every corner. He repeated some mantras. Don't analyze the process. Become the process. Let the process manifest its truth. Accept its truth.

He held his breath for four counts, than 8, then twelve. The pain he never consented to was over. Lorraine's sudden mood swings and accusations, they were over. The desire for her was leaving his body. The hunger for her was leaving his mind. He expanded his chest and sucked in oxygen until he felt its chilly tentacles in his vagus nerve.

He was holding his breath in for almost three minutes when a voice broke his trance. He sat up and saw a figure dressed in a hooded lime-green puff jacket talking excitedly into a cell phone a few yards away. Dane got back on his feet. One of his legs had fallen asleep so he shook it wildly then dragged it along.

"You alive?" a man shouted from the green hood. He sounded high. "FUCK! YOU ALIVE?!"

"I'm quite alive, thank you," Dane said, trying and failing to speed up his pace so he could pass him quickly.

"I thought you was dead." The man walked closer.

"I'm fine, I just needed to rest." Normally he would be chagrined if someone caught him acting weird in public. He was too numb from brain to ass to give a shit what anyone thought. Tonight he had finally become a real New Yorker.

The man started clicking his cell camera.

"Really?" Dane said. "You're going to Instagram me?"

"I thought you was shot in the head and bleeding out!" the man shouted. "You were thrashing around like a whirly-dervy, and then you died. I saw it. Not a breath out of you. I thought I was hallucinating when you got up. Did you get shot?"

"Blood?" Dane looked down and for the first

time saw a thin streak of blood staining his shirt. He reached up to his temple and realized that the hot coal he felt earlier was another vicious wound inflicted by those god damn roses. It must have happened when he fell on them in Jax's cab. His temple was throbbing and swollen, the source of all his head-pain.

"No, not shot. Sorry if I worried you, I'm fine," he tried to act polite, though he was too pissed to feel polite. He just wanted to get home and climb into a warm bath and drink wine and read a Kindle and call in sick to work tomorrow.

"Fine? You fine? How? I seen you die!" The man waved his arms, "You want 911, man? I'll get you 911."

"I said I'm fine," Dane said gruffly.

What else would happen to him tonight? Would he get run over by a bus? Or maybe get stabbed? Why not? The guy probably had a knife. Men who hang out on street corners in the middle of the night always carried weapons, didn't they? Dane craned his head up and down the avenue while the man kept talking loudly into his cellphone. "He was dead, Aces, I'm saying he was dead as a doorknob."

A cab suddenly appeared out of nowhere and rolled to the curb.

It was Jax! Holy God in Heaven, it was Jax. He broke into a run and the guy behind him started yelling, "Get back here, I'm not done talking to you yet. I want to know how you died and got back up. Are you an angel?"

Dane hopped into the cab as fast as he could. "OMG, how did you find me? OMG, what a relief. Did Booker call you?"

"You're lucky you have a friend like Booker looking out for you," she said. "What were you doing, lying on the sidewalk?"

"Resting."

Jax checked her side-mirror and accelerated. They drove along silently. Dane didn't know what, if anything, she knew and he didn't know what, if anything, he could tell her.

Jax kept her eyes glued to the road. It was like she had lost all interest in him since their first meeting. He wished she would talk to him, if only to get him out of his own head. In fact, he wished she would just keep driving, flooring the gas pedal as they passed his exit, gliding along to the north, and making the wide curving turn onto the George Washington Bridge to speed to the Palisades and beyond.

If only she would do that, just drive into the night as far from everything and everyone in New York. That would be perfect. He wanted to run away, like when he was a kid and would start walking out of town, all the way to the highway, trudging along the shoulder of the road while pick-up trucks whizzed by, only to return a few hours later, pretending he never meant to leave in the first place. Only this time he wouldn't come back. Jax could just drop him in the middle of nowhere and leave him there. That would be fine by him.

Jax spoke quietly: "I decided to eat my second gyro near the club, outside a coffee place I like, Cafe Grumpy. You know it? Then Booker called and I drove back to the club and sat outside, reading my Kindle. I saw you come out looking like a ghost and watched you stomp that bouquet to death." She wagged her head. "I didn't know a person could hate flowers that much." She paused and sipped from her thermos. "I lost sight of you at the dumpster. Did you throw something away?"

Dane sank into the shadows of the back seat, blushing so deeply he couldn't bear for her to see him. It was probably Jax who passed him when he ducked behind the dumpster. "It was a gift for Lorraine."

"Lorraine who's really Loretta," she said.

"So you know!" A long slow wave of emotion swept over him like a foreign life force. He whispered. "You know."

"Booker said your friend Geoff called him to check on you and filled him in. It's not the first time I've heard a story like that." She met his eyes in her mirror.

"I always wanted to meet a woman as fucked-up as my mother," he tried to make it sound like a joke. Then the truth slipped out. "I hate her."

"Lorraine or your mother?"

"Both!!" Dane snarled.

Jax moved into the right lane and turned onto the 72nd Street exit. Snow was falling heavily now and city salt-spreaders and snow plows were mobilizing. An army of rumbling equipment idled near Riverside Park, tying up traffic up and down the block and creating bottleneck conditions. Jax headed south to detour around it, driving slowly up a neatly-plowed side-street.

The streets and buildings glittered in raiments of frost. He wanted to unlock the door and hurl himself from the vehicle. He wanted to roll on the ice and feel nothing but ice. He needed to feel its freezing intensity. He needed its pain to stop feeling his pain.

His hand paused on the latch. A dark undertow lapped at his soul, drawing him into an eddy of confusion. He had nothing to live for. Booker didn't need him. No one really needed him. He wanted to let go and let death swallow him up.

The cab turned left onto Broadway. The bright lights crept into the car, blowing it up with shadows like a fun-house. He put his hands in his lap and bent his head. He was desperate for a joint, a glass of strong wine, a pain pill, maybe all three.

Unthinkingly, he wailed. "I thought she was the one! With a capital O. Well, I'm done. I'm fucking done with it all. Fuck BDSM."

"BDSM isn't the problem," Jax said as if she'd been expecting his outburst. "The problem is people who lie and play games, but those people are everywhere." Her tone was matter of fact. "There is no one One. There are lots of ones who could make you happy."

Dane wiped his eyes with his palms. He tried to make sense of what Jax was saying. It reminded him of Booker's metaphor about the river of life. He had tangled with a blood-sucking barracuda when he thought he'd caught his forever dolphin. It was strangely comforting to see it that way.

"Yeah, okay, but I'm done fishing for a Mistress," he grumbled. "I'm too fucked in the head."

"Are you?" she said, "That's not what Booker says."

The Ansonia's towers shimmered in the distance. He wasn't so bad off if he had a beautiful, kind, rich man waiting for him at home. He didn't need a Mistress. He could always play with his crew at the club, and at home, he had Booker all to himself. If they turned from a two-some into a threesome, so what, it would feel even more like a family.

Jax pulled over to a fire hydrant and let the car idle while she turned around to face him. She was even prettier than he'd realized. She had a high forehead and wide lips. Her eyes sparkled and that dimple was killer cute.

"Can I level with you?" she asked.

"Well, yeah. Sure," he said uncomfortably. He wanted to know what she wanted to say to him, but at the same time he was afraid of a lecture.

"There are patterns in life, some of them real and some of them simulations. Like a real pattern is everyone sleeps. Right? We all need sleep, we all stop doing things and lie down to sleep and wake up hours later and start the pattern over again. It's everyone's biological reality."

This wasn't what Dane was expecting. He was baffled. "Right…"

"Right, so a simulated pattern is, say, a businessman waking up every day to do more or less the same things other businessmen do, wearing suits and ties, commuting to offices far away, having meetings, taking lunches at the same time, and going home when the sun goes down, right?"

Dane agreed with her again. "Right."

"But that isn't a real reality. It's just a post-industrial simulation of reality."

"Are you a Matrix fan too? I love the Wachowskis!" Dane said.

Jax sighed. "Let me finish, I promise there is a point in here somewhere!"

"Yes, Ma'am!" he said meekly, his lips twitching with amusement.

"A person like Loretta Linguini exploits simulations."

"It's Lanzetti, for Christ's sake, not Linguini. That's practically racist." Despite his protest, he started laughing. That's what he'd call her in his head from now on.

"Shut up and listen," Jax ordered. "You bought into the simulated image of dominance. A manufactured image filled with assumptions about how a dominatrix should look and act, how she had the right to be a selfish, graspy bitch, and all that is bullshit."

"What did Booker tell you?" Dane didn't realize Jax knew so much about him.

"He told me enough," she said, "Enough to know you were victimized, even if you don't see it that way yet."

"No, I do," Dane murmured, "I do, now."

"The lesson from this is not that you give up on BDSM. You can't give up who you are or stop needing what you need inside. That won't work, Dane." Her head shook back and forth. "Trust me, that does not work."

"I know," he said softly. "I know it doesn't."

"BDSM is real people, 3-dimensional people, not fantasy people. Regular human beings, some of them good and some of them bad."

Her voice grew as loud as her convictions. She was scolding him. Yet it didn't feel bad. It felt, well, the only word he could think of was "real." The way Brian had been totally real with him tonight. Brian was right to level with him, to treat him like a grown man who can take a hit and still keep going, to respect Dane enough to know that he would fight his way through it the way he'd fought through everything else in his life.

He appreciated what Jax was saying. She wasn't telling him what to do. She was just telling him he needed to do things differently.

"You're right, I attached more importance to how she looked than how she acted," he admitted. "My fault. I consented to it."

"No you did not. You did not consent to being abused. Look, I don't know you yet," she said in a voice as sweet as honey. "I just hate seeing a guy like you get hurt."

"A guy like me?"

"A sub guy. It's not fair."

He didn't know what to say. "Thank you. I'll be okay, really. I'll get over this."

Jax put the car in drive and pulled back into traffic. He angled himself so he could see her in the rear view mirror. Her strong face was filled with emotion. He wished he knew what she was feeling. Her face fascinated him. Her lips looked ripe and sensitive, her eyes darted from left to right as if she was constantly solving life's math problems.

She double parked outside the regal entrance to the Ansonia.

"Are you married?" Dane asked.

"That's random," Jax smiled. "I'm married to my dogs. Not legally, of course, but we're permanent partners."

He didn't know anything about her, or why Booker felt it was okay to talk openly to her about his relationship with Lorraine. Kevin the florist said everyone knew Jax. Who was she?

Another cab pulled up behind them and honked impatiently.

He pulled out his wallet, trying to think of a way to delay his departure. He was thrilled knowing that Booker was waiting just a few flights away. Still, he wished he'd spent more time asking Jax about herself and her interests.

"Booker already covered your fare and then there was that nutty tip you gave me." She waved at the driver behind her to pass her but he kept honking. "You better get out. That driver is a jerk."

Dane didn't want to move. "You saved my life tonight. Maybe even literally."

"All in a dom's day's work. In the future, please don't lie down on city sidewalks in deserted parts of town in the middle of the night when it's winter outside," she said. "With your luck you'll get frostbite and your nose will fall off."

"Would you see me again?"

The cab behind them sat on its horn. Jax gave the driver the finger.

"You know, like a date?" Dane asked.

"Like a date or an actual date?"

"An actual date! We could go to sushi place that opened on 75th."

"I know a better one," she said.

"We'll go there," Dane said with a bounce.

The cab driver behind them had stepped out of his car and was making his way towards them.

"Get my number from Booker and get out of the cab, NOW," Jax ordered.

In seconds, Dane was on the sidewalk with his backpack, seconds from the door to the castle he lived in. His head pain had lifted and the welt in his pants was just a dull throb.

Linguini was dead to him now. She was in jail, a prisoner of her own bad character. He, on the other hand, would soon be in his happy bubble, eating fresh ginger breads and snaps and partying with two wonderful men who would pamper him all night if he let them. And he just scored a date with an amazing new woman.

He lingered on the sidewalk a moment as icy winds blew down Broadway. They cut through him with an exhilarating sharpness. Plumes of steam shot out of manholes, making them look like active volcanoes. The glare of snow-machines made the avenue as bright as day and the grinding of their motors roared like synthesizers. Pedestrians packed the streets, wandering into restaurants and vanishing into the subway. The world was so alive. He had so much to live for.

Wait. Did Jax say she was a dominatrix?

৪১ Books by ৪৩
Gloria G. Brame

BDSM EDUCATION

One of the world's most qualified and prominent advocates for the acceptance of BDSM as a legitimate expression of human sexual desire, Brame was lead author on the classic book, *Different Loving: The World of Sexual Dominance & Submission* (1993, Random House), called the "bible" of BDSM and widely-hailed as the first major academic effort to normalize BDSM and Fetish sex, 25 years later, *Different Loving* has become a landmark text in the global study of BDSM.

Different Loving, *Come Hither*, and *Different Loving Too*

Gloria's three masterworks on BDSM/fetish draw on thousands of in-depth interviews and clinical case studies. Together, these three books provide a comprehensive education in the realities of being kinky, including what BDSMers do, why they do it, how they do it, and what they think about it.

Different Loving

This 1993 breakthrough in sexual literature is a complete, comprehensive guide to and tour through the world of masters and slaves, fetishists and other BDSM lifestyles.

Available on Amazon: **http://amzn.to/2eg0u3z**

Come Hither

If you've ever wondered about the ins and outs of bondage, spanking, or cross-dressing, look no further. *Come Hither* is a frank, reader-friendly guide on how to turn your kinky fantasies into satisfying expressions of love and desire. Quizzes and fun guides inside.

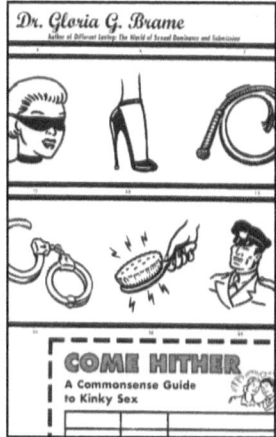

Available on Amazon: **http://amzn.to/2e6xGXD**

Different Loving Too

The ultimate companion to the original *Different Loving*, *Different Loving Too* is a fascinating update on the secret lives of BDSM people, and how attitudes and science in the 21st century have both changed the way people both understand and live out their BDSM needs. Includes polls, new scientific data and studies on BDSM, and follow-up interviews with 19 people from the original work. Readers new to BDSM will find this a bracingly honest look at a still taboo subject. Experienced BDSMers will be delighted by the refreshing candor and profound true-life stories of people who have truly been there and seen it all.

Available on Amazon: **http://amzn.to/2faDArX**

SEX EDUCATION

The Truth About Sex is a trilogy explaining the science and history of human sexuality and how sex actually plays out in real life. (Third volume coming in 2020.)

Vol 1, Sex and the Self

One of the most cited sex books in the world, this volume was the first to introduce a comprehensive list of the scientifically-correlated health benefits of orgasm. A re-education in factual sex for teens and adults, this volume covers the repressive history of sex ideology, and explores the science of human sexuality. With non-binary, self-empowering models for sexual fitness and chapters on the psychological importance of sexual consent, *Sex and the Self* is a groundbreaking work that will change your life. *Includes a friendly guide to self-pleasure for all genders.*

Available on Amazon: **http://amzn.to/2gldRkY**

Vol 2, Sex for Grown-Ups

Challenging common notions of normality, this volume rejects patriarchal views of sex, including the out-of-date Kinsey Scale, and offers original models of sex and gender diversity based on Dr. Brame's long experience as a sex researcher and professional sexologist. Based on hundreds of clients' stories, and a wealth of research on the history and science of sex, this volume demonstrates that human sexuality is a living, continually evolving part of life. From the fundamentals of sexual intimacy to fetish formation, BDSM, polyamory, and LGBTQ, this book uses 21st century facts to prove that diversity is the true norm. *Includes a creative guide to sex techniques for all genders.*

Available on Amazon: **http://amzn.to/2efTyDw**

Erotic Awakening (E-book only)

Throw away the pills, potions, and struggles and tap into the sexy person you really are. Learn how to integrate mind, body, and spirit using the evidence-based techniques for erotic re-awakening that have transformed the lives of thousands of clients in Dr. Brame's private practice. We all experience cultural training that tells us what we shouldn't do - instead of showing us how wonderful it can be when we know exactly how to harness our sexy side. That's where Gloria steps in: in a culture where myths and inhibitions about sex keep adults perpetually blocked from their true erotic potential, this guide will tell you the facts about sex, give you exercises to bust out of inhibitions and anxieties in bed, and show you how to blossom into the satisfied sexual adult you were meant to be. Packed with clinically-tested tools and exercises to relax and re-awaken your primal energies, this e-book is for ALL adults, regardless of age, gender or orientation.

Available on Amazon: **https://amzn.to/2zG9xEZ**

MEMOIRS

Naked Memory

This uninhibited memoir paves a new path in female sex history, fearlessly depicts the rocky road that faces sexually unconventional teenage girls. From naive assumptions to shocking revelations about sex, from the first awakenings of lust to the reckless travels through strangers' beds, *Naked Memory* shines light on the radical adventures of a very kinky girl.

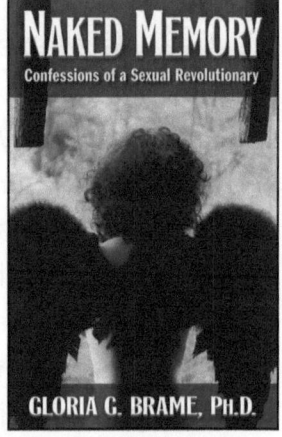

Available on Amazon: **http://amzn.to/2fohqat**

A Fetish for Men

Based on her personal essay, Growing Up Kinky (Huffington Post, 2017), Gloria's second memoir recounts her harrowing teen years, from political activism during the late 1960s to sexual trauma, in the 1970s, all against the background of her life as a child of Holocaust Survivors and her struggles with queer, non-binary and kinky identity.

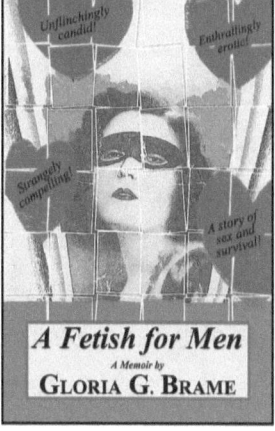

Available on Amazon: **http://amzn.to/2e6x3NP**

ໝ About the Author ༄

Gloria G. Brame is an award-winning, American board-certified sexologist and sex therapist. Her private practice specializes in consensual BDSM, Fetishism, Kink, gender identity and sexual health. Dr. Brame's forensic work assists lawyers and courts  with expert assessments of kink-related sex crime cases.

Brame is also a best-selling sex writer, radical sex educator, outspoken advocate of sexual freedom for all consenting adults, and personally allied with the BDSM, fetish, and LGBTQ communities. Her groundbreaking books on the history and science of sex are of value to anyone who appreciates the broad variety of human sexual experience, from self-pleasuring to esoteric practices.

In 1987, Brame founded the world's first online BDSM support group (on Compuserve). In 1993, she published *Different Loving* (Random House, 1993 and 1996), a landmark academic study of BDSM. In 2000, she completed doctoral studies in BDSM/Fetish sex (Ph.D., IASHS). Since then, she has published 9 other books on the science, history and human realities of sex and gender, provided invaluable sex education for adults on her blog, and hosted or founded a dozen BDSM membership groups, chats, and other environments for the discussion of kink.

Brame's Internet presence includes her website **gloriabrame.com**, a sex positive compendium of writing, advice, and professional services; the *Ask Me Anything* professional BDSM/Fetish blog on Reddit.com (2014, 2016); The Leather Hall of Fame, where she sits on the Board of Governors; and BED: Brame's BDSM Educators Directory. She has been cited in such online outlets as The Huffington Post, Slate, VOX, and VICE, among others.

Follow her on Facebook, Twitter, Amazon, GoodReads, LinkedIn, Alignable, and other social platforms.